A MEMORABLE OCCASION

A Memorable Occasion

by

Nara Lake

Dales Large Print Books
Long Preston, North Yorkshire,
BD23 4ND, England.

British Library Cataloguing in Publication Data.

Lake, Nara
    A memorable occasion.

    A catalogue record of this book is
    available from the British Library

    ISBN   1-84262-244-7 pbk

First published in Great Britain 1978 by Robert Hale Limited

Copyright © Nara Lake 1978

Cover illustration © Melvyn Warren-Smith by arrangement
with P.W.A. International Ltd.

The moral right of the author has been asserted

Published in Large Print 2003 by arrangement with
Mrs Ellen J Waye, care of Juliet Burton Literary Agency

Dales Large Print is an imprint of Library Magna Books Ltd.

Printed and bound in Great Britain by
T.J. (International) Ltd., Cornwall, PL28 8RW

One

Rowland Radford, usually called Harry for
some reason everyone had long since
forgotten, saw Helena for the first time in
the parish church near his brother's English
home.

Harry was the youngest of the Radford
brothers by many years. The eldest, Richard,
considered that he had made a sufficient
fortune, and about seven years previously
had retired to an estate not far from his
birthplace. For Richard Radford, this
combined two things, a pleasurable return to
the scenes of his boyhood, and triumph. He
had purchased the Hall from the bankrupt
heirs of the bankrupt squire to whom he had
touched his forelock as a youth.

Naturally, the local gentry gazed askance
at Richard Radford, who was rough, bluff
and grizzled, a man who had conquered
part of the Australian wilderness and acted
like it. At sixty, he still nursed ambitions, but
was realistic enough to know that he and his
wife would never break into county society.

Comparatively late in life he had married a woman many years his junior, and he now pinned his hopes upon his children, seeing to it that they were better educated than himself. For them, the way up had to be through marriage. There were always plenty of gently bred people with good connections and no money. The established English practice of primogeniture saw to that, and he was aware that there were many young men and women happy to exchange breeding for security.

His two younger brothers, who with him had sailed across the Bass Straits from Van Diemen's Land to the southern portion of the Australian mainland now called the Western District of Victoria, preferred their adopted country. The Radford brothers were three of the seven children of a poor farm worker who had gone to Van Diemen's Land as the servant of a man who hoped to make a fortune there. It was the servant who had prospered, and when old Radford had heard that there was good land for the taking in the new district centred about the village of Bearbras (Melbourne), he had immediately sent Richard, Robert, and the boy Rowland, to join in the grab.

So the Radfords chose their land without

regard for the law which emanated from Sydney, hundreds of miles away, not caring that they were dubbed 'squatters'. They knew that the government could not afford to dislodge them, or others of their kind. The wool from the flocks spreading out across the wide lands was now the mainstay of the economy in New South Wales, and the squatters, tough men prepared to shoulder the hardships, and the risks, were able to call the tune.

Twenty years later, the colonial governments made bumbling attempts to dislodge the squatters from their big leaseholds, but the same gold rush which had brought in emigrants hungry for land had enriched the squatters too. The new laws, meant to wrest away land from the wool barons, were full of loopholes, and men smart enough to build up fortunes out of virgin country soon found them. The land laws played right into the squatters' hands by giving them the chance to purchase – in a somewhat roundabout way – the land which they had held as tenants.

The Radfords, who had three separate leases, but worked jointly under the 3-R brand, were not slow to seize upon these weaknesses in the land legislation, and by the mid eighteen-sixties held freehold the huge domains they had taken from the native blacks over a quarter of a century earlier. They owned a vast sweep of volcanic plain extending from the central Victorian mountain ranges to the white sands bordering the Bass Straits, with the exception of one patch behind the sand dunes, a three hundred acre minuscule owned by a certain Wesley Eggert.

This infuriated Harry Radford. Good grazing land had been alienated, and worse still, access to portion of a small river which flowed behind the dunes for some miles before emptying into a lake which in turn emptied itself over a rocky bar into the ocean. Wesley Eggert was a former gold miner who had struck it sufficiently rich to pay cash for his 'selection' at the absurdly low price set by the government. Unlike so many of his fellow selectors, who, when they found themselves the subject of all sorts of persecution from their squatter neighbours, were glad to sell out at a profit, he clung stubbornly to his land. Wesley Eggert was unable to make much more than a bare subsistence living from his land, and the Radfords often wondered how he managed to survive at all, but they acknowledged that for sheer stubbornness, few men were his equal.

Even thirteen thousand miles away, in England, Harry Radford thought occasionally about Wesley Eggert, and tried to devise fresh ways of easing the selector from the land he honestly considered his own. *He* had been the first to tread it – if one excepted the blacks and certain mysterious castaways – and he remembered vividly the day, blustery yet fine, like so many in that part of the world, when he had ridden out from the hut he shared with his elder brother, to search for some missing sheep. He had forded the river, low in late summer, and more out of curiosity than anything else, had climbed to the top of the dunes, to make two very interesting discoveries.

One was that, out to sea a few miles, there stood a strangely flat-topped island, a mesa rising out of a plain of water. Teenaged Harry was a little less pragmatic than his brothers. He could sometimes look at land and think of it as being pretty rather than as a base for grass which in turn fed stock. There was not much time for imaginative flights whilst pioneering a sheep run, when one was forever watching out for marauding blackfellows, or the diseases which crippled

11

the sheep, or the bushfires in summer, or flash floods, or, depressingly, weevils in the food. Nonetheless, he stood for quite some time and gazed out across the sea at that island, weaving a silly fancy or two about it, and from thenceforth, he thought of it as 'his view'.

The other discovery was the wrecked ship. He saw it for the first time that day, and only once again, when it was fleetingly revealed after storms had blown away the sand which had buried it. Where had it come from? How long had it been there? Was it just a sealer blown up high by a furious gale, or could its origins have been more romantic? A Dutchman sent out to explore New Holland which had found itself adrift in the turbulent waters north of Van Dieman's Land? Or a Spaniard? They said the Spaniards nearly found Australia once, sailing from Peru in search of the Pacific's lost souls, to bring them safely into the True Faith. Some of those tiny, highly decorated caravels had vanished, and according to the history book, had never been seen again.

Harry would not have admitted these daydreams to anyone. Publicly, to his family, he said that Wesley Eggert was a damned nuisance, sitting there in the middle of the shore end of his run, so that he had to take his stock round the confounded fellow's fences instead of straight across. Privately, he felt that Wesley Eggert had stolen both his view and his mysterious ship, which no one had sighted now for fifteen years.

To anyone meeting Harry Radford for the first time, it would have seemed unlikely that there was a romantic streak in such a man. When he met Helena Clayton, he was thirty nine, nudging middle age, every inch of his solid six feet of height telling the world that he was a successful man-on-the-land. His brothers retained their provincial English accents, but Harry had a marked colonial twang. He had been six years old, the baby of the family, when his parents and their tribe had set out on the almost interminable, acutely uncomfortable voyage to Australia, 'tween decks on a slow old tub whose steerage quarters still reeked of the wool carried Home last trip.

He had seen two of his sisters buried at sea, along with other fever-stricken offspring of their fellow passengers. With such searing memories of sea travel implanted into his young mind, it is little wonder that he had delayed his trip Home for so many years, although well able to afford it since he was twenty. In truth, he would have been quite content to stay in Victoria. He was someone there, a rich man who stayed at the Melbourne Club when he was in town, and with two terms in the Legislative Council behind him.

The force which had pried him out of his happy niche of vast grazing lands and local importance was a sudden desire to provide himself with legal heirs. There had been a couple of servant girl mistresses earlier, and there was always female companionship of an impermanent and undemanding (emotionally, if not financially) nature in Melbourne when he had to stay there for his parliamentary or business duties. It was his sister-in-law Ailsa, wife of the middle Radford brother, Robert, who had prompted him to decide upon the drastic step of matrimony. He had considered the subject from every angle, taking in the fact that his comfortable, rambling house, added to as the need arose, would not do for a wealthy married squatter, and that he would need a larger household staff than the married couple who now tended his wants. It would be goodbye to those gay spells in Melbourne, for although he had not stood for re-election at the last polls, he managed to find business in town whenever he felt like tossing his wide-brimmed hat over the windmill.

If Harry had been able to stand Ailsa, he would have gone unmarried to the grave. Ailsa, Robert's wife, was the daughter of a Melbourne publican who had become very rich during the gold rush, and it seemed to Harry that everything that was unpleasant about the newly rich was contained in her short, bustling person. She was a snob of the worst kind, ingratiating towards those she wished to impress, patronising or rude to those she considered beneath her, a cruel gossip, and a shameless social climber.

What was naïve ambition in Blanche, Richard's wife, came across as a clawing battle to reach the top in Ailsa. It annoyed her that Richard, after long years of grief for a sweetheart who had died young, had married at forty eight, and that his nursery was now stocked with robust youngsters. Still, Richard and his brood were in England whilst she dwelled only a few miles from Harry, who surely must prefer her own growing children to those nieces and nephews halfway across the globe.

Ailsa had never forgiven her husband's eldest brother for marrying, and she carried this over into an intense jealousy of her amiable and fecund sister-in-law. When Richard bought his splendid house in England, she was not satisfied until Robert consented to build a new house for her. She obtained plans of Richard's mansion. So, he had twenty bedrooms. Well, what Blanche had, she would have, only better. Robert Radford's new homestead was the wonder of the Western District, and outdid all others erected by the wool barons. It was identical in every respect to Richard's – except that everything was larger. The rooms were three inches longer and the ceilings a shade higher, the main staircase had three extra treads, and the terrace was much wider. Thus, when it was completed, visitors could gape and note that a hundred yards behind this vast new piece of eighteenth century architecture was a large farmhouse which had been quite adequate, and beyond that again, the tottering split timber shack which had sheltered the Radford brothers for several years.

With this triumph to flourish, Ailsa began talking frankly of those days when her children would own everything from the central Victorian mountain ranges to the sea. How she would persuade Richard to give up his run, managed now by his brothers, to provide the mountainwards stretch, Harry did not understand, but he did grasp the significance of the seawards side. He would have to die.

And it could happen, any time. A fall from his horse. He had broken his arm two years earlier when he had tripped over his gig after too much to drink. It could have been his neck. And what about illness? There was always typhoid going the rounds in towns, and even Prince Albert had fallen prey to this deadly infection. Then, there was that nasty bushfire they had experienced in '62, and only last year poor Malcolm Harris had been shot by a half-crazed bushranger who had bailed up his homestead.

Harry, actually, was not childless. There was a young girl boarding at a Melbourne convent whom he acknowledged as his daughter, and he had things tied up so that she would never be in want. But his heiress. Never! Most likely, she would turn into as big a fool as her mother, now married to a man as Irish and Catholic as herself, and with so many children that the mind boggled. Harry knew where his responsibility lay, but he was not stupid. Garranbete, to which he had given his youth and hope, was not going to Ailsa's children, but it would not be left to young Colleen, either.

Having made up his mind to marry, he looked over what his friends vulgarly called 'the field'. It was unsatisfactory. There were nice young things of eighteen, daughters of the men who had pioneered these rich lands concurrently with the Radfords. They made him feel ancient. Besides, too many of those eligible young ladies were Presbyterians of the sterner variety, and to put it bluntly, Harry did not wish to share his bed with a Calvinist. Ailsa was a fair sample of the breed. Poor old Robin had to sneak out to the old shack to smoke, and woe betide him if she smelt the demon drink upon his breath. He decided to extend his search abroad, visit England, 'overseas', as he called it.

Before he left, he arranged to have a new stone house built, on the rise behind his present abode, so that one would glimpse the sea from the upper windows. It would not be as grandiose as Robert's mansion, but enough to settle any reasonable woman contentedly.

Harry travelled in style, luxuriating in his own stateroom, by the new steamer route to Suez, enjoying the sights of Ancient Egypt on his way across the desert to another steamer at Alexandria for the last lap. He took his time, dawdling through Italy and France and buying up an immense amount of furniture and bric-a-brac to ship back to the new house at Garranbete, ready for a bride he had not yet met.

There were flirtations on the way, but nothing came of them, and as the year he had allowed himself for the exercise drew to a close, he settled down to enjoying himself in the company of his eldest brother's family. It was odd to be staying in a house so like that of his brother Robert, and yet it was immediately obvious to him that there is always a difference between original and imitation. Richard's house had been lived in for several generations, and possessed that subtle thing known as atmosphere.

Outside, the grounds offered another contrast. Back in Victoria, Ailsa had sought advice from the Government botanist, and his recommendations stood dotted across the cleared earth, supported by stakes and still carrying their smeared and inky labels. Here, the gardens were bursting with a thousand delights, and enchanted the visitor as he explored, usually accompanied by a small nephew or niece. Remembrances of early childhood, smothered by the years, emerged as he smelt the blossom and helped little Elizabeth gather wildflowers in the hedgerows.

Spring in Victoria was a patchy affair of wild rainstorms, golden flashes of wattle blooming in the scrub, and native flowers which were often protected by hard and prickly stems or leaves. Then, just as the land gained its ultimate green and looked almost English, the sun, rising towards the summer solstice, scorched it all into typical Australian brown. Yet, Harry was homesick, and longed to go home to Garranbete.

Unlike Richard, who had been a grown man when he had emigrated, leaving behind the sweetheart who had died before she could join him, Harry had only hazy recollections of his homeland. The harsher landscape was the norm to him, and its threats and challenges so much a part of him that he sensed that this beguiling prettiness of burgeoning apple blossom, bluebells in the coppices, and neat fields each contained by its hedgerows, would eventually soften and change the man he was.

He told his family that he would soon be leaving them. He wanted to see how his new house had shaped up, and more importantly, to check on the welfare of his stock and the general management of his run.

'What a shame you weren't here during the hunting season,' said Blanche. 'All our best young women are off to London for the Season now.'

Harry knew that Blanche meant well, but he was irritated, nonetheless. Even if *the* Season had been held right here in the local village, it would not have made much difference to the Radfords. As he had discovered during a sojourn in London, rich Australians rated for nothing more than curiosity value. Everyone thought that their fathers – and mothers – had been convicts in chains, and the fact that most of those who had become rich had gone out to New South Wales as free settlers seemed quite unknown.

And he was not sure whether he wished to take as wife a hearty young woman who took her pleasure thudding across the countryside on horseback. He had in mind something gentler, more feminine. It would be useful if she could ride, but he did not care much for women who aped men. In London, he had learnt all about the 'pretty horsebreakers' with their hard good looks and high prices, but they were somewhat apart from strapping young women who forced their horses over well-nigh impossible jumps and watched the hounds tear in for the kill.

'I must go home,' he said, not wishing to admit that he had failed in the prime purpose of his journeyings. 'I can't expect Robin to manage everything for me much longer.'

Yet, the next day, he met the young woman destined to be his wife.

Harry was no churchgoer back in Victoria. Like most squatters, he read prayers to those of his employees who happened to be near the homestead of a Sunday, but he seldom bothered with a ten mile ride to the nearest Protestant church, which was Non-conformist, whereas the Radfords were nominally Anglican. He was always hospitable towards any clergyman of any denomination who called at Garranbete whilst on a parish round which could extend over a hundred miles, but, although no agnostic, he had little real religious inclination. Ailsa was inclined to go on and on about the dangers lurking in nearby Wicklow, centre for local small farmers, many of whom were Radford tenants, and who were predominantly Irish. As long as they paid their rents and behaved themselves,

Harry did not care where they went on Sundays.

Back in England, he discovered, to his surprise, that Richard, who had always been as easy-going about religion as himself, attended church regularly. It appeared that living in the big house brought with it a built-in obligation to attend the parish church.

Two

On this occasion, Harry Radford, having been the last of the Radford contingent to enter the old Norman church, was seated next to the centre aisle, and so found himself separated from, but in a line with, a tall, slender, very white-skinned young woman. She had heavily waving dark brown hair, unpadded, he judged, and her straw hat, he noted, was quite a little older than the sprigs of artificial flowers and small ribbon bows which now decorated the band.

Settled down for a sermon about sin, which, like most sermons, only touched upon this interesting subject in a hypothetical way without giving any actual examples of what to avoid, Harry kept allowing his gaze to roam in her direction. There, he decided, was an attractive woman. Not really pretty, and well into her twenties, but with a certain style about her. She wore gloves, so that he could not find out whether she was single, engaged, or married, and once when she realised that he was looking at her, she turned away quickly and lifted her chin into the air.

Well, well, he thought, amused, and yet put out, I'm not as bad as all that.

His fair hair was as thick as it had ever been, and so far untouched by silver, his sidewhiskers were fashionably trimmed, and even if his skin had become a little lined and weatherbeaten, it was of the kind which tanned rather than reddened, so that his grey eyes always appeared light and bright in his face. He was heavier than he had been at twenty five, but still very fit and well-knit, and in his new London clothes, he considered that the reflection he had seen that morning in the cheval mirror had been definitely prepossessing.

When they both arose to go to the communion rail, he had the opportunity of discovering that she was single, for, of course, she had already removed her gloves. She did wear a ring with a small ruby on her right hand, but none on her left.

Outside, after the service, Harry asked Blanche the name of the young woman.

'Oh, that's Helena Clayton, the vicar's daughter,' replied Blanche, indifferently.

'Clayton?' The vicar, known better in the district for fox hunting than soul saving, was definitely middle-aged, but Mrs Clayton was scarcely thirty.

'His daughter by his first wife,' said Blanche, as if to an idiot. 'She's only a year or so younger than Mrs Clayton.' She looked at her brother-in-law curiously, and without approval. 'She's a governess. Or was. She came home suddenly this week. A quarrel with her employers, I heard.'

Richard took her arm to escort her to their carriage, at the same time admonishing his two youngest daughters for their frisky behaviour.

'Introduce me,' commanded Harry, in a low and suddenly intense voice.

Blanche stopped dead, and stared at him. She did not think much of Miss Clayton, one gathered. Like Ailsa Radford, she had been well-off for most of her life, if hardly out of the top drawer, and she thought that her brother-in-law was going beneath himself. Still, she was good-natured, and so, after a shrug, she smiled.

'Clergyman's daughter, not your style,' muttered Richard in Harry's ear. 'Poor as mice, the lot of 'em, and proud as the devil into the bargain.'

Harry believed the last. He had seen the made-over hat and the tilt of the chin. It pleased him. He liked a woman with fettle, and at the same time, that determination to keep up appearances touched his heart.

Although a slightly puzzled frown passed briefly across Miss Clayton's face, she allowed herself to be introduced to Harry, who, because Blanche was being formal, was named as Rowland Radford.

Close up, and in bright daylight, Helena Clayton was still very white-skinned, milky, thought Harry, allowing his mind a little play about what extended below that demure neckline, though with the faintest scattering of freckles across her very presentable nose. Her eyes were a hazy grey-green, the colour of the Bass Straits when one stood on the sandhills and looked out towards flat-topped Lady Julia Percy Island on a cloudy day. She was not a great beauty. There were little imperfections like a slightly crooked front tooth when she smiled, and her bone structure was such that she was better in profile than full face. Her figure was good, and even allowing for her tight lacing, her waist was small under a delicately swelling bosom. The hands he had noticed earlier were long-fingered, which was supposed to be a sign of good breeding, and her wrists slim, which augured well for her legs and ankles.

Her smile was brief, no more than formal. She did not seem interested in the Radfords' visitor from Australia. Harry made a couple of remarks about how pretty the countryside was at this time of the year, and how he had enjoyed her father's sermon, which was an outright lie, because he had been so absorbed in studying Miss Clayton that he had soon lost the gist.

She murmured something in reply, and he said bluntly that he hoped that they would meet again, soon. She seemed a little startled, and then, after a small nod, moved off in the direction of the church hall where, it seemed, she was about to take a Sunday school class.

'Of course,' remarked Blanche, as they were driven home, 'it must be hard for Miss

Clayton. She and Mrs Clayton don't hit it off, from what I've heard. Oh, nothing really, but you know how it is sometimes. Mind you, she's a very – well, reserved, I suppose you'd call it – person. She was engaged, you know. To an officer in the Indian Army. She still wears his ring on her right hand. He was killed in one of those horrid little wars they have out there. Not the Mutiny. Since then. About a year ago, wasn't it, Richie?'

Richard did not know. He did not listen to all the village gossip as did Blanche.

His wife was not deterred by this oblique reference to her essential vulgarity.

'Yes, a year. A few months after the poor Prince died. He died right at the end of the year – Prince Albert, I mean – and Helena Clayton was preparing to go to India to be married. It was just before Agnes was born. I remember now. She was most dreadfully cast down, poor girl. You can't blame her. It's no fun being a governess.'

Harry chewed this over whilst strolling about the grounds that afternoon, puffing on his pipe, which Blanche treated with the utmost abhorrence. Lor', he brooded, how women carried on about smoking. Sniffing the air as if it had been poisoned, sending the master of the house into exile in a special room, making him wear a smoking jacket so that he would not make his other clothes smelly, and one of those fool Chinese caps, to keep the fumes from his hair. Women were such hypocrites. Plenty of the lower class kind smoked quite openly, and he suspected that many a genteel female tried it out on the quiet. Perhaps he'd do best staying single, after all. Young Dick, Richie's eldest lad, wasn't a bad little chap. Perhaps he could come out to Garranbete one of these days…

No, he had come overseas for a wife, and at least, he was going to make an honest try. This Miss Clayton was the first suitable candidate he had met who genuinely attracted him. He could visualise her as mistress of Garranbete, softly spoken, a perfect lady, never letting her refinement slip as did Ailsa, or Blanche, who was not above garnering village gossip from the servants.

So, she had loved someone else, and would have been long since married if the poor fellow had not died. Well, that showed that Miss Clayton was not a born old maid, likely to have convulsions if a man put his hands on her. Besides, Harry pondered realistically, treating the matter in the hardheaded fashion of a man who never bought an animal without looking into its bloodline, she was in her late twenties, and less likely to be fussy about things like a colonial accent, humble origins, and ... um ... Colleen.

He called at the vicarage early the following afternoon, and was told by the maidservant that Miss Clayton had gone out walking. Mrs Clayton, flustered, still youthful, but already harried by the cares of a household where there was never enough money (and too much of their income was absorbed into the vicar's passion for hunting), then appeared. She was taken aback when she realised that the big, handsome man who had been staying with those commonplace Radfords at the Hall had called to see her stepdaughter.

'When will she be back?'

'I don't know, Mr Radford.' He had the feeling that Mrs Clayton was trying to work out the best course to take. She wanted to look down her nose at him, but at the same time, he was well-to-do, and she must have known that he was interested in Helena.

Then:

'Lena – Miss Clayton – had a headache.

She said she'd walk for a while to try to clear it.'

To Harry, time had become very precious.

'Could I catch her up? Which way did she go?'

Mrs Clayton again hesitated, but after a pause told him that Miss Clayton had taken the left turning in the lane. She liked to walk that way. There was a view from the hill at the end of the lane.

Harry saw her before he reached the hill. She stood near a pond in a meadow, the breeze billowing her skirts, and causing her to hold on to her hat.

'Hullo,' he called, climbing over the stile. 'Do you mind if I join you?'

She turned, obviously interrupted in the middle of a reverie.

'I...' Then she stopped, as if unable to think of anything else to say.

'I'm sorry if I'm intruding, but it's pretty here.' Harry walked to her side. 'Funny thing, but every so often I remember little bits of when I was very small. I came from these parts, you know. I think I came here once. My father was a shepherd, you know.'

He was not sure why he said such a thing. It was rather as if he wanted to put all his cards on the table. She kept a straight face as he talked, and he remembered how Blanche had described Helena Clayton, whom she hardly knew, but whom she judged by village gossip. Deep, that was the village opinion of the vicar's eldest child.

At the same time, he was not unaware that Helena Clayton had been studying him with those hazy eyes of hers, as if trying to make up her mind about him.

'And, do y'know,' he continued, 'it's been a surprise to me about shepherds. Y'see, where I come from, a shepherd is about the lowest man there is. Crawling after sheep, they call being a shepherd. But here, it's a decent profession.'

'How interesting,' she said, and then, abruptly, after several seconds' pause, 'Have you been to the top of the hill? The view is quite excellent.'

'No, but I shall go to the top of the hill, on condition that you show me the way.'

There was just a hint of a smile at the corner of her mouth, now.

'You only need to follow the lane,' she answered.

'I'm a stranger, here, Miss Clayton.'

Now she did smile, and she fell into step beside him, but her eyes did not change, and he felt a strange flicker of unease. What did the villagers mean by deep? Then he dismissed the fancy. She was a shy young woman. That was all. She reminded him of someone, though, and it was not until late that night, alone in his room with a contrarily smoking lamp, that he recollected just who it was. A woman in a painting he had seen in Paris. Of course, it had not been the original, just a good copy. He'd nearly bought it, too, only he thought the price a bit steep for an imitation. Some Italian fellow had painted it hundreds of years ago, the original, that is, and the smile had been rather like Helena Clayton's. A lot behind it, with the eyes giving nothing away.

A week later, he asked Helena to marry him. They were out riding, on horses he had borrowed from his brother, with a groom at a circumspect distance behind.

'This is rather sudden, Mr Radford.'

'But it ain't a surprise, is it? You must know I wouldn't be chasing you like I've been unless I had marriage in mind. You aren't the sort of … well.' He stopped, mid-sentence, feeling that he was moving on to dangerous ground. 'Look,' he said, 'let's go back and have tea with my sister-in-law. Then we'll talk about it in the garden.'

He was very truthful with her. He told her

that he thought that she would make him a suitable wife, and that he was sure that love would grow between them. He also mentioned Colleen, and it did not seem to matter very much to her. He went on to say that he knew that there had been another whom she had loved dearly, and at the end of all this talk, she accepted him.

The worst of it was the stiff interview with her father, who frankly considered a colonial far below the Clayton family, which had tenuous connections with some of Britain's best families, although, thought Harry cynically, there had not been much money handed on with the blue blood.

Richard wished him well. He said he considered Miss Clayton a quiet sort of woman who would never give Harry much trouble. Blanche was less kind.

'You're the best chance she'll ever have, Harry. She's an out-of-work governess. Do you know how many out-of-work governesses there are in England, Harry? Thousands! I've heard that she stayed on in London for a little while after she'd been dismissed, looking for a new post. But who'd have her? If she was stupid enough to quarrel with her employers, she didn't get a character, and no one hires anyone without a character, Harry.'

Harry wondered, not for the first time, what the quarrel had been about, but when he asked Helena, again, she dismissed it merely as a difference of opinion. It puzzled him a little. Helena did not seem the argumentative type.

Still, the wedding went off well, with a lavish breakfast provided afterwards by Richard and Blanche, for Eudora Clayton, Helena's stepmother, was pregnant again and was unable to cope, or so said Helena's father. Harry kept his thoughts on this to himself. For all their airs, the Claytons could not have afforded much more than tea and biscuits, and Eudora's indifferent health was a piece of face-saving.

In due course, the newly married couple were driven to the nearest railway station and installed in a first class carriage with a large hamper just in case they had not already eaten enough. Harry tipped the guard generously so that they would not be disturbed (he had already taken the precaution of reserving the whole compartment) and settled himself comfortably across from his bride, who sat there quietly in the eyes downcast fashion expected of her. If he had been alone, he would have taken off his coat and put his feet on the seat, for he had had a fair amount of wine and was a little drowsy, but he guessed that sort of sloppy behaviour, which had been his normal back home at Garranbete, would offend Helena. She edged along so that she was sitting next to the window, looking out at the green countryside.

'Do you know,' she said, suddenly, 'that this is the first time I have ever travelled first class?'

'There's always a first time,' he answered, cheerfully.

Now, neither of them could think of anything to say, and Harry felt panic sweep through him. What had he done? He had tossed away nearly four decades of happy freedom, that's what he had done, and for what? The chance to put Ailsa's nose out of joint, that's what.

'Would you like some wine?' There was a bottle in the hamper, still chilled.

'No. Thank you, but no.' Her voice sounded a little strange, and she kept her face determinedly away from him as she continued staring out of the window.

He saw her reflection in the glass, and the glisten of tears on her lower lashes. He was appalled, and hastened to set matters right.

'Lena!' He stood up, and as the train lurched, fell rather than seated himself alongside her. 'Now, what's wrong, eh? Homesick already?'

He made her turn towards him, and he thought, what the hell's the matter with me? She's what I've been waiting for all these years. He bent his head and kissed her on the mouth, with none of the restraint he had practised over these past weeks. For a second, barely longer, her lips were cool against his, and then she sighed, and responded with a passion so violent that it was as unexpected as it was delightful. Harry felt her arms tighten about him, and noticed that her new hat had toppled from her head and was on the floor, undoing her carefully arranged hair as it fell, and he began laughing.

'Lena, Lena,' he whispered, kissing her again and again.

Married life was going to be wonderful.

Three

Every so often, Wesley Eggert left his small holding in the care of an acquaintance, and headed east for Melbourne. It was a tough journey, part of the way on foot to the nearest coaching station, thence to the railhead, and from there to the capital. These excursions were a mixture of business and pleasure, for, as with most bush bachelors, a spell in town meant cramming a year's dissipation into a few days.

Wesley was thirty-two at this time, a lean young man of medium height, with hazel eyes some called wild, and a rather weak mouth hidden by his full beard. Yet, in spite of that mouth, he could be astoundingly resolute, and to match his stubbornness, he had a wiry physique which had not yet deteriorated under the onslaughts of his drinking bouts. He belonged to that breed which stays sober sometimes for months, and then seeks complete oblivion in the bottle for days, until forced back into sobriety by the imminence of delirium tremens.

He had not always possessed this weakness. A decade previously, he had landed in Victoria full of the crazy hope which had brought thousands to the goldfields. Unhappily, he and his young wife and child had arrived during the slump which had followed the first insane impetus of the gold rush, and during their wretched months of near-starvation, he had bitterly regretted the dull but safe post he had held as a clerk back in London. Finally, he started earning wages as a 'digger' up at Bendigo goldfields, but in 1856 his wife and child had died of typhoid fever within a week of each other. He had been completely heartbroken, and had never recovered emotionally or mentally from the blow.

Still, life had to go on, and some time later he took advantage of the new land acts to select for purchase from the government a block of land on the vast acreage still leased by the Radford brothers. His farming was of the learn-as-you-go variety, yet, as time went past, he was more concerned in keeping to himself than tilling the soil. The land was too boggy for sheep, lying as it did alongside a river flowing behind the coastal dunes as it sought a way to the sea. It was, however, suitable for cattle, and with a small kitchen garden and a few fruit trees near his timber shack, he felt himself quite satisfied. For a change of diet, there were always fish in the river, and the occasional duck brought down by a shot from his old flintlock. The trips to Melbourne broke his routine of scratching a living, fighting a running war with Rowland Radford, and yielding periodically to his craving for liquor.

In nearby Wicklow, the hamlet which provided the district with postal services, religion, liquor, general merchandise and provisions, and not very satisfactory schooling for the robust crop of young Irish-Australians, there had been some conjecture as to how Wesley Eggert remained solvent. One day, the licensee at the Donegal Arms made so bold as to ask Eggert outright.

The recluse, who, as usual was drinking alone, stared at him from bloodshot, but still shrewd, eyes.

'Gold. Struck it rich.'

Then he had thumped the bar to attract the attention of all the other drinkers.

'And don't any of you Irish spalpeens come to my house lookin' for it!' he yelled, on the edge of one of his dangerous rages. 'I'm not such a fool as all that. That's why I go to Melbourne.'

After he had gone, the patrons of the Donegal Arms ceased their usual discussions over Home Rule, Vinegar Hill, Oliver Cromwell and all the rest of it, to debate the source of Wesley Eggert's income. He must, they all agreed, have put it safely away into some sort of investment up in Melbourne. A queer character was Wesley Eggert, but not such a fool as he looked. And you had to hand it to him. While all the other small farmers were paying out rents to the Radfords, he was a freehold landowner.

The man he left in charge during his absences was as much a misfit as himself, or rather, one of those peculiarly adapted misfits who were to be found in the Australian backblocks. The name of this man was Adolphus Fisher, and he was the child of a union between a white sealer and a Tasmanian native woman. He was short and skinny, with putty-coloured features of European cast, topped by a curly negrito mop of greying hair. A knock on the head during a brawl some years before had left him what the locals called 'a shingle short', given to lapses of memory and slightly deaf, but he was a diligent worker. Because he was a little dull, he was happy to perform

41

such unpopular tasks as thistle cutting (Scottish thistles, brought accidentally into the country, had turned into a curse), and clearing away the lumps of volcanic rock which littered this part of Victoria.

'Dolly' Fisher had one especial attribute, and that was boundless good temper, and he was almost the only person thereabouts who had any sort of friendship with the taciturn and unpopular Wesley Eggert. He was also pathetically honest, and Eggert had no qualms about leaving him in charge of his few head of cattle.

When 'in town', Wesley always stayed with Mattie Baxter. Mattie was an old acquaintance of his goldfields days, when she had run a sly grog tent from which she had profited greatly. In those days, she had been a sprightly, girlish figure, astonishingly youthful for her thirty years, and had in her charge a little girl to whom she referred as her niece. The uncharitable cast doubts upon this claim, for Mattie was as well-known for her lovers as for her sly grog tent. For once, the uncharitable were wrong. The little girl *was* her niece, left for a fortnight whilst her parents sought their fortune elsewhere. They never returned.

Mattie comforted Wesley after his darling

Molly and little son died. If she had not been already married to a scallywag who had bolted with two month's takings soon after the wedding, Wesley might have taken her to wife, simply because he needed someone. After her unnerving matrimonial experience, Mattie had been more careful with her money, and now lived very comfortably in Melbourne on rents from the property in which she had invested. Her own house was just large enough to permit her to offer hospitality to old friends like Wesley.

Eggert's visit to Melbourne followed the same pattern as over the past two years since he had settled in Western Victoria. He executed his business first, and then went on to Mattie's. She expected him, for he had written warning her of his advent.

The front door of the little two-storied house in fashionable Fitzroy, a near-Melbourne suburb, was opened to him not by the mistress of the house, resplendent in the flashy finery which made her better-bred neighbours wince, but by a slightly, dowdy-looking girl in her middle teens. He knew her, of course. It was the niece, Katie Foster, who was generally known by her aunt's surname, Baxter.

'Hullo, Katie,' he said, curtly. He did not bother to add that she was looking grown up. It was no surprise. Last year, she had been fifteen. This year she was sixteen, which was the age at which most girls started to be young adults. Privately, Wesley thought she had not improved much, not a patch on her buxom aunt, for as so often happens when a girl lives with an over-poweringly determined and sensual older woman, Katie was colourless and somewhat lifeless.

From force of habit, he patted Katie's cheek as he passed, not seeing the sudden spark in her eyes, nor the angry stiffening of her small frame. Just then, Mattie appeared in the drawing-room door, surrounded by her enormous skirts, and with her beringed hands held out towards him.

'Wes, love. My colonial oath, it's good to see yer!' She smelt, as ever, of gin and cologne, and he embraced her with a hint of passion. Good old Mattie. Always there. No strings. Just a lot of fun.

Katie went off somewhere else, and then Wesley realised that there was another man in the drawing-room, looking daggers at him. Still, they all sat about and drank gin, and because Wesley was not in his black drink-himself-into-oblivion mood, he merely sipped at his glass.

'Time you went, Con,' said Mattie then, giving the other man a playful tap on the knee, and he left, with obvious signs of unwillingness.

'Runs the pub along the street,' explained Mattie, leaning back luxuriously when she and Wesley were alone, and fanning herself. At the same time, she undid a couple of buttons at the top of her bodice, although the May day was quite cool, it being autumn in Melbourne. 'Thought you'd be 'ere earlier, Wes.'

'Had some business,' he rejoined curtly. Wesley did not wish to talk about his business while Mattie's expansive bosom was so enticingly obvious.

'That's what you said last time you was in town.' Mattie pushed his hand away. 'Wes, let's talk for a bit. It's good to see old friends, y'know.' She uttered a gin-laden sigh, and took up her glass again. 'Yer think yer troubles 'll go away as yer gets older, but it's the opposite, Wes. They gets worse.'

'Money?' He hoped that she did not expect him to help her out of any fiscal trouble.

'No. That's the least of me worries, Wes.

Now, you met Con. He's me licensee. I *own* the pub.' Here, Mattie paused for a few seconds, enjoying the self-satisfaction of her worldly success. 'No, Wes, I ain't worried about money. I'm nicely fixed. It's Katie.'

Wesley could not imagine what meek Katie had done to distress her flamboyant aunt.

'She's man mad,' said Mattie, sounding utterly mystified, as if she could not for the world of her understand why such a nasty trait had surfaced in a close relative of hers.

'She looks scared of her own shadow,' commented Eggert, still not very interested.

'She only looks scared. She's the worry of me life.'

'Girls go through a stage. She'll settle down.'

Mattie finished her gin, grimacing to show the intensity of her worry.

'Oh no, Wes. It's not a stage. It's not just – well – boys. It's – it's got so I can't 'ave a man friend in me own 'ouse.'

'Katie?' He was astonished. Ever since he first remembered her, Katie had been a miserable little mouse of a child. Even when quite small, she had been inclined to hide from visitors, peeping out shyly, and, as she usually had a running nose, not very appealingly.

'Now, take Con O'Brien. That young fellow you met just now. It's got so I don't like 'avin' 'im 'ere to talk about business. And we need to talk, sometimes, Wes.'

Eggert was absolutely sure that Mattie had other things on her mind besides business when Mr O'Brien called, but he made no comment. He wondered whether she was trying to make him jealous, but he was long past such feelings about Mattie. Rather, his attitude was one of disimpassioned interest. Con O'Brien was a good looking young fellow. Probably grow as fat as a pig, like most of these publicans, but for now he was handsome, with his high colour and black hair and Irish blue eyes.

'She flings 'erself at 'im, Wes. Con's decent, but he's a man like the rest of 'em. One night, last week, 'e came round while I was out, visiting some lady friends. That young devil came to the door in her nightdress, nothin' else, improper as you like, and asked Con inside. Just as well I came 'ome when I did! I'm tellin' yer this, Wes, to warn yer. I want yer to stay 'ere, like you always does, but it's up to yourself if you'd rather stay somewhere else.'

Eggert assured Mattie that she need have no fear. As far as he was concerned, Katie was still a little girl, and he had been looking forward to this stay for weeks. But he immediately began thinking of Katie in a different way.

It was, of course, a clear case of chickens coming home to roost, and Wesley noticed for the first time that Mattie was definitely middle-aged. Now he came to think of it, Mattie was quite a few years older than himself. It had not mattered before, but this visit Mattie was looking her years. Going to bed with her no longer seemed so desirable, and he decided to have some more business in town.

'This business of yours – what is it?' Mattie cocked her head to one side, bright eyes narrowed, and a stray beam of sunlight came to rest upon her hair, which until then had looked naturally golden. 'You certainly keep it to yerself.'

'An investment I got.'

Eggert noticed that Katie had just gone out of the front door. If he hurried he could catch up with her. Katie, eh? As they said, still water runs deep.

Katie was standing at the omnibus stop near

the corner of the street, which was also outside the public house which Mattie owned. Eggert saw the licensee inside behind a window, glaring out at him as he spoke to Katie, and he felt like laughing. Con O'Brien could have Mattie all he wished. *He* was set to explore a bit of new territory.

'Going into town?' he asked Katie, who stood there silently, clutching her basket, her small face pale beneath her cerise bonnet.

'Yes, Mr Eggert,' was the prim response.

'Mr Eggert. I used to be Uncle Wes. You're old enough now to call me Wes.'

'I'd rather call you Mr Eggert.' Was she being prudish, or teasing him?

'We'll have to change that, won't we?'

The omnibus rattled to a halt with a clatter of hooves and wheels. As soon as it stopped, Katie hopped aboard, skirts bobbing, and he jumped up after her. There were two vacant seats. One was near the front of the conveyance, the other near the entrance at the rear. Katie promptly chose the latter, leaving him to lurch forward and fall heavily into the vacant seat, narrowly avoiding the lap of an enormously fat woman of uncertain cleanliness. They jogged along to

49

the next stop, where two more intending passengers came aboard, and Katie, just as the omnibus moved off, leapt out on to the roadway, narrowly avoiding a horse and its rider. The horse shied, and a burst of virulent language followed Katie along a narrow side lane.

Wesley tried to rise and follow, but his way was blocked by the two new passengers. He was annoyed, knowing quite well that Katie had done this to give him the slip, but at the same time, his interest was further aroused. Playing hard to catch, was she? They'd see about that.

The next three days followed the pattern of his stays in town, with a great deal of drinking and roistering, but it was easy to sense that Mattie had lost her old verve. It was not only that she was looking her age. Even in their most intimate moments, her mind seemed to be elsewhere, and Wesley calculated that elsewhere was the licensee of her public house. He found himself able to study the situation with cynical detachment, gaining more amusement each time Mattie remembered that she was out of gin and needed to run down the street to replenish stocks.

He placed Con O'Brien's age at no more

than twenty-five, which made him about fifteen years younger than Mattie. Well, it was Mattie's funeral, and it meant that her attention was away from Katie. Well, partly away from Katie.

'Just like a little animal she is, over the men,' lamented Mattie. 'If I didn't watch over 'er night and day, she'd be out on the streets.'

Wesley, by this time, was agog with curiosity. He knew that Mattie resented having a practically grown up niece to draw attention away from herself, but her efforts to warn him against Katie had, of course, the opposite effect. It had reached the stage where he had to find out what lay behind that timid, pallid, little face.

On the fourth morning of his stay there was a dramatic early morning scene. For some reason, Con O'Brien had chosen to call at the ungodly hour of half past eight, and Wesley dragged himself out of bed as the shouting below grew louder and more angry.

'If I catch the little slut hangin' round you again, I'll belt the daylights out of 'er,' screeched Mattie, who was hungover and nervous at that time of day. 'If, if I gets an 'int, one 'int, Conan O'Brien, that you've

51

bin encouraging the little tart, I'll see to it you lose your licence, and every shred of yer reputation.'

O'Brien laughed raucously, confident of his position as young lover of an older woman.

'Reputation. Come off it, Mattie.'

They both became aware of Eggert at the head of the stairs, and quietened, looking up at him. O'Brien's face flushed angrily, and Mattie, still in the tatty splendour of a lace-trimmed velvet gown she wore in her leisure moments, slid her arm through the publican's.

'Oh, Con, love,' she cooed, 'don't let's be bad friends. Katie's not worth it.'

However, as was to be expected, O'Brien was enraged by the sight of his rival in a nightshirt, and took a step forward as if to charge up the stairs. Wesley, no stranger to catch-as-catch-can fighting, reached instinctively for an ornamental vase which stood atop of an occasional table, and then saw that he was not alone. Katie stood there, in a bright plaid dress, her face swollen with tears. With a choking sound, she turned and ran into her room, slamming the door. Wesley picked up the jar, and stood ready, while O'Brien, thinking better of being caught at such a disadvantage in a fracas, backed to the front door.

'I'll see you tonight, Con,' Mattie called after him in a tremulous voice as the young man hurriedly left the premises.

'What was all that about?'

Wesley had come downstairs, after dressing hastily. Mattie sat at the breakfast table, lifting a cup to her lips with a shaky hand.

'Oh, Wes. It's 'er. Came sneaking in, she did, just as I come down. Said she'd bin out to buy bread.'

'Had she?' Wesley drank his tea, quickly. It helped get rid of the foul taste in his mouth.

'There was bread in 'er basket. But it was the look of 'er, Wes. She hadn't 'ad a full night's sleep.'

'Why did O'Brien come into it?'

'Con came round to ask me to the theatre. Tonight. You don't mind, do yer, Wes? You could come too, sit somewhere else. 'It's "East Lynne", a really good play. Can't leave yer 'ere with Katie. She was 'anging round the door of the pub when Con came out this morning. Worried 'im sick, it did. 'E keeps an orderly 'ouse.'

If Wesley had been thinking clearly, he would have realised that the pieces did not quite fit, but now his mind was racing ahead to the night. All right. He would go to the theatre, but he would be back again like a shot. Tonight, he would find out about Katie's limitless hunger for men.

It went marvellously well. While Mattie, dressed up for her night out, waited for her escort, Eggert left for town and the theatre, even going to the expense of hiring a cab to make it more convincing. He went to the theatre, and studied the names of the cast on the posters outside, so that he could talk intelligently about them the next day.

Katie was not at home when he arrived, but he heard her later, closing the front door and creeping up the stairs. However, as she passed the door of the darkened guest room, which he had hardly occupied since his arrival, he heard her humming under her breath, a sweetly gay little tune. He waited another ten minutes, to give her time to undress. The maid was asleep in the small room downstairs at the back of the house, or should have been, and Wesley, supremely confident, walked across the passage to Katie's room.

She thought that she was alone upstairs, and had left her door slightly ajar. She did not instantly notice that he had pushed it open, for she was sitting in front of her small mirror, clad in drawers and chemise, peering at her reflection with all the absorption of the young female discovering for the first time that she had certain charms. She touched her lips with a finger-tip, caressingly, uttering a little sigh. Then she knew that she was being watched, and she turned, startled, and then frightened as she saw Wesley Eggert's face staring at her with a naked avidity ill-concealed by his beard.

'What are you doing here? Get out!'

'Stop playing games, Katie.'

He grabbed her, and she struggled furiously with all her slight strength. He flung her on to the bed, which was neat and pristine under its white coverlet, and then fell on top of her. She screamed, and he killed her scream with his mouth, biting into her lips as he took her.

When it was all over, and he lay panting face down at her side, conscious of her choking sobs, a truth floated out of all the lust and battle. Katie had been a virgin, and he had raped her. Oh my God, he thought. What have I done?

He had no time to work this out, for Mattie's voice was cutting through the room.

'So this is what goes on when my back is

turned,' she declaimed, and he saw that she had with her their servant, and another woman, a reasonably respectable neighbour with whom she occasionally played cards.

'Oh, my darling!' she cried then, running to embrace Katie, who, still crying, was staggering to her feet. But Katie ignored her and stumbled to the neighbour.

'Take me away,' she implored, taking the startled woman by the arm. 'Just take me away.'

Mattie was now all flint and resolution, whilst Eggert, embarrassed beyond belief to find himself with this feminine audience, tried to dress himself.

'I'm going to call a policeman,' said Mattie.

'Now, see here…' blustered Wesley Eggert.

Everything, he thought, had gone crazy, but he knew that nothing he said would make any difference. Mattie had trapped him, and as he rode homewards in the train a week later, he knew why. Conan O'Brien was interested in Katie, and Mattie was interested in O'Brien, who had certainly not invited her to the theatre on that particular evening.

Wesley, the occasional lover, had arrived in time to be used for the purpose of removing

Katie, who sat beside him now, deathly pale, the saddest young bride ever to set forth with a new husband.

Oh yes, Mattie had been clever. She had laid her traps very carefully, and he, fool that he was, had raped a young girl of good character. Mattie had put it to him, plainly, that unless he married Katie, the law would intervene. Katie had wept and complained, but she was told by her aunt, just as plainly, that if she had a baby, she might as well have a legal father for it.

Wesley, sitting in the train, thought of Maria, his dead wife, and their beloved child, and then he remembered the goodness of their life together and contrasted it with the ugly squalor of his relationship with Mattie Baxter. He wanted to be sick. Why had he left himself drift like this? It was the booze, of course, but he knew that as soon as he reached home, he would drink until his body could endure no more, just to blot out the whole agony of it. He looked out of the window at the rolling paddocks dotted with sheep, fat with fleece against the green, and the trees and occasional homesteads as the train chugged away from Melbourne across the plains. He had to keep on looking out, to conceal the unmanly tears he felt prickling under his lids.

At his side, Katie ate out her poor broken heart. She had been so happy when she had returned home that night. Conan O'Brien had been at her for weeks to leave home. She could go to his sister's, and he would arrange for their marriage. He didn't care about the licence of the pub. He'd soon get another. That humiliating scene early in the day had made up her mind for her. Returning from the bakery, she had met O'Brien, who had walked her to her door. Then Mattie had flown out, berating them both, screaming in her best Billingsgate, and Con had pushed them both inside, so that the whole street would not be an audience. At last, Katie conquered her fear of her aunt, and told Con that she would do as he wished.

Instead, she had been hustled into marrying this horrid, half-mad man whom she had feared ever since she could remember. Her aunt told her not to worry. It would not be as bad the next time. But it was. He was cruel and violent, hating her as much as she hated him, and using his body to avenge himself on her, on Mattie, and the whole world.

Four

A rough looking sailor acted as interpreter, and after some discussion with the *concierge*, the old woman, her gold earrings providing the only colour in her overall drabness of ancient black rags and sallow skin, led the well-dressed foreigner inside, leaving the interpreter to pocket the coin awarded him for his services, and amble off towards the nearest tavern.

The crone must have felt curiosity about her new tenant, who had only a long, narrow, leather case as luggage, but except for a few mumbles and gestures to indicate that he must follow her, she said nothing. For one thing, he would not have understood her Marseilles patois. For another, she had lived in this harsh waterfront world for so long that nothing surprised her. If she thought anything of the reason why this quietly attired, sinewy man with red hair should require a room on the top floor of the stinking tenement she managed, it was that he was a sexual pervert. Whenever a person from 'outside' came to these sordid lodging houses, it was for some sinister and underhand purpose. She only hoped that he would not accidentally hang himself, as had one visitor a decade ago. It had brought the police around, which scared the life out of her other tenants.

The new lodger stepped into the room to which she had unlocked the door. It was, as far as rooms of its kind went, fairly clean, and saved from the stench of lower floors by reason of its elevation. He went briskly to the window, stood there for a moment, his eyes narrowing, and then nodded, and gestured that he wished to be left alone.

She shuffled away, and he closed the door. Then he sat awhile on the edge of the bed, and after one or two resigned prods at the hard mattress, stood up again. Now, he unpacked, unlocking his case with a key taken from an inner pocket of his American-styled jacket. He tossed an English newspaper to one side, and lifted out a pair of field glasses in their own case. Almost as an afterthought, he shot the bolt on the door, and went again to the window. Almost the only good thing about this wretched room was the view, taking in as it did a large part of the harbour.

The day was still, clear, and yet shimmering under the heat of an early summer sun. The warmth worried him, and this was not surprising, for the room was directly under the roof. He took out a handkerchief and mopped his forehead, gritting his teeth in disgust.

Despite the flush caused by the heat, he was a quite prepossessing individual, with bright blue eyes and brows unusually well marked for a person of his colouring. His features were a little too craggy for good looks, and one profile was marred by an irregularly shaped scar about three inches long just above the jawline, and emphasised, rather than concealed, by the whiskers he wore trained across his cheeks, meeting in a well-trimmed moustache over a firm mouth. In dress he was precise without being foppish, and an observant person would have concluded that there was something military both in his bearing and array. This was correct. He had reached the rank of major in the Union Army during the late war between the States in North America.

There was no reason why he should not have continued his military career, for which he was absolutely suited, in the war against the Indian tribes of America's west, but there was much distasteful to him in the idea. He saw the Indians as underdogs, victims of Anglo-Saxon ambition. So, now he was in another army, without uniform, and depending upon the generosity of well-wishers for his living expenses.

Somewhere, a bell tolled the hour. It was two o'clock, and Marseilles was about to stir from its midday somnolence. Down at the Napoleon Dock, no more than a few hundred feet from the watcher high up under the eaves of this ancient tenement building, workers moved slowly back into life. One ship, however, seemed exempt from the usual attentions of dockyard workers.

The most modern of her kind afloat in the year 1867, she sat sleek and trim in her berth, whilst her complement of marines drilled on her forward deck. The vessel was Her Majesty's Ship *Galatea*, and although her masts were bare, and her twin stacks smokeless, Major Doyle, as he swept her with his glasses, could see that every square inch was being kept up to that spick and span tradition of the British navy.

Yet, all was not well on board. An enforced stay here in Marseilles during the whole of the month of May had had disastrous effects upon some members of its crew. The harbour was sheltered from the fiercer winds blowing across from North Africa and down from the Maritime Alps, but it was also the receptacle for untreated sewage pouring from the ancient drains of this very old town. Various illnesses had struck down many of the *Galatea,* some cases proving fatal, and morale was low. This *'Vieux Port'* was old in Roman times: two thousand years of insanitary conditions had made a cesspool of the modern dock.

Major Doyle turned away from the window, set down the glasses, and re-opened the case. He removed a baize cloth, and exposed a rifle, in parts, so that it fitted neatly into the prepared compartments of the leather case. Smiling slightly to himself, he began assembling the rifle.

This done, he walked back to the window, aimed at a spot on the gangplank which bridged the gap between the quay and the *Galatea,* and, satisfied, placed the weapon on the floor beneath the bed, and began his wait.

The heat gathered under the roof of the old house, beating in through the tiles, until the red-haired man, sweating profusely, and unable to endure more, unbolted and opened his door. There was a small window cut into the wall opposite. He had already observed this, and it was one of the reasons why he had chosen this room. The window opened out on to the roof, which in turn butted against the flat roof of the next building. Here was a useful avenue of escape. So, he struggled with the ancient casement which had not been touched for years, and when it swung open, went back into his room, leaving the door open to provide a through draught. This made conditions a little more tolerable, and to pass the time, he read the newspaper.

Three o'clock. Any time now.

He took up the rifle, and loaded it carefully, uttering something in a tongue that was not his usual American-oriented English. Then he pulled a rosary from a pocket, and, closing his eyes, slipped the beads through his fingers. The beads themselves were unusual, each carved from bogwood.

He was ready for this, the supreme moment of his life. During his years of hard fighting in the field, he had never felt such an intense sense of dedication. If by chance, he had found himself marked out to perform a deed of unusual heroism, upon which the fate of the Union could hang, he would have slipped into the history books by accident. This was his emergence upon the stage of history, not by a fluke, but through deliberation.

He was startled from this state of near ecstasy by the clatter of hooves upon the cobbled streets below. He had allowed a quarter of an hour from the railway station. They must have taken a short cut.

He kicked the door shut, and poised at the window, fixing his sights exactly upon the halfway mark of the gangplank.

Those on board the *Galatea* had similarly been caught unawares by the early arrival. The guard rushed out to take up their places, the master-at-arms cracked out orders, and a seaman tugged at the rope which would hoist the standard aloft.

The commander of the *Galatea* had arrived back from his official junketing through France up to Saxe-Coburg-Gotha, and the pleasure on the guard's faces was not entirely because the men were pleased to see their captain again. His return meant that they could be out to sea, away from this pest-hole, before the next day passed.

The commander, a slight, dignified figure,

but at the same time strangely boyish to be carrying the responsibility for the crack naval frigate, left his carriage, and the usual saluting and ceremonial began.

The man high up in the tenement had his sighting perfectly aligned. His finger tightened on the trigger, and as the commander of the *Galatea* stepped on to the gangplank to be piped aboard, the door behind Major Stephen Doyle was flung open. The old crone stood there, her toothless mouth agape, her bright black eyes astounded and accusing.

She began yelling at him in her unintelligible patois, and he lost his chance. The commander was aboard, amidst men, behind cover, and the British Royal standard had fluttered to the masthead. His Royal Highness, Prince Alfred, second son of Queen Victoria, fourth in line to the British throne, and heir-apparent to the rulership of tiny Saxe-Coburg-Gotha in Germany, was quite unaware that he had just miraculously escaped assassination.

The concierge was not so lucky. Major Doyle's flattened palm caught her side on, across the throat. He had killed men twice her size and a third of her age in this way. He heard the crack as her neck snapped, and when she had fallen to the floor, he stood very still for a moment, straining his ears for any sound of movement elsewhere in the building. There was none, and without haste, he took his rifle to pieces, repacked it with his glasses into the case, and went down the stairs in a casual and leisurely manner. He met no one.

The concierge's grandson informed the police that his grandmother had, when he had called on her earlier, expressed her doubts about the Englishman who had rented the attic room. (All English-speaking persons were English to her.) Although given to minding her own business, she feared that he was one of those queer specimens from *Angleterre* who can gain satisfaction only by hurting themselves.

By then, Major Doyle was on a train headed for Paris, and from thence, Calais. He was deeply disappointed, but planning anew. The *Galatea* was off on a world tour. There had to be another place where he could await the royal sailor, who was the most vulnerable and accessible member of the British ruling house. To strike so deep into the Saxon oligarchy would do more to help his native land than all the talk, all the muddled rebellion, and all the melodramatic idiocy of such schemes as attacking English gaols. When one attempted to kill a hydra, one sought to strike the body, not to remove a head which automatically replaced itself. The assassination of a Royal prince would hit right at the very heart of England. The oppressors would know then that no one could be safe.

It was the sight of a devout peasant woman in the corner opposite, lips moving silently as her fingers caressed her beads, which caused the first fears to pass through the outwardly impassive Major Doyle. His fingers felt inside his coat, and an image danced before his eyes. The old woman lay on the floor. He packed his case. But the rosary, the one precious family possession he owned, the sacred object which, he believed, had protected him through the long years of bitter war, lay still on the bed, beneath the week-old copy of 'The Times' he had not bothered to take with him.

The policeman who picked up the rosary from the top of the bed asked the grandson whether he had ever seen it before. He had not. In due course, the rosary came into the hands of a police inspector, who, when he had examined the object closely, decided to take it to an expert on religious matters. This learned abbé had been at school with him, many years before, and was pleased to help.

'But, Claude, *mon ami*. This is most unusual. Look here.' The abbé had taken a magnifying glass from the top of his desk, and he held it so that each bead was enlarged. 'Study, I beg you, the larger beads. I never thought to see such a thing – see the carving, the pictures.'

The inspector, not a very devout man, but one with certain principles, crossed himself.

'Sacrilege. Pictures on the beads of a rosary?'

'*Non, mon vieux*. These are copied from the Book of Kells, one of the greatest treasures of Christendom. This treasure is now kept safely in Trinity College, Dublin. These little figures, Claude, have been copied from the illustrations of the Gospels. Imagine, a book a thousand years old. And every page a hymn to the glory of God. Those old Celtic monks, Claude, kept the best of our Faith alive during the darkest days in Europe's history.'

'Then this comes from Ireland.' The inspector was now very thoughtful. 'If it's as precious as you say, our murderer may try to recover it.'

'The rosary itself isn't valuable,' pointed

out the other. 'But it could have great sentimental meaning to the owner. But Claude, don't you see the significance? An Irish rosary, a British warship in our harbour, a dead woman in a room overlooking the Napoleon Dock.'

The policeman picked up the rosary and dropped it delicately into the large palm of his left hand, looking down at it, and shaking his head.

'An Irish assassin. Of course. The English Prince Alfred returned yesterday. What do they call those crazy terrorists? Feni – Fenians.'

'From the old Irish word *fianna*, meaning soldiers,' interpolated his erudite friend. 'Or, sometimes, these Fenians prefer to call themselves the Irish Republican Brotherhood.'

The two men stared at one another, their fertile Gallic minds leaping about all the dreadful possibilities which had been so narrowly averted. This young Alfred, commander of the *Galatea*, now sailed to other parts, was he not also a German prince? A member of the British Royal Family murdered upon French soil was bad enough. A German princeling, at a time when Prussia was seeking to dominate a

Europe of which France was rightfully the foremost nation...

'I think, *mon cher Claude*,' murmured the abbé, 'that the death of that old woman has saved us from the worst scandal ever to rock Marseilles.'

Five

The Radfords had to go to Melbourne during September, 1867. The matter had arisen suddenly, from a letter Harry Radford received, written by the mother superior of the convent where his daughter had spent most of the past ten years.

'She wants to become a nun,' said her father, despairingly, handing the letter to his wife, who sat reading her own English correspondence, brought that day from the nearest township of Wicklow by the mailman.

Helena raised her finely marked dark brows. She was surprised, for Harry had told her several times that he feared his daughter would become as flighty as her mother. She kept her ideas on this to herself. It had been quite all right for Colleen's mother to be flighty when it had suited Harry, but daughters, even illegitimate ones, were a different affair.

'There's nothing for it,' said Harry, heavily, 'but to go up to town and talk this over.'

He had always been utterly frank about Colleen to his wife, and Helena had met the girl once or twice during visits to Melbourne. These encounters had not been entirely comfortable, but both sides had done their best, so that relations remained amiable.

Harry went alone to the convent to talk with Colleen. The girl, whom in earlier years he had considered almost as rattle-brained as her mother, had developed a sudden, new maturity. She was seventeen now, and, thought her father, aptly named, for with her thickly waving dark hair, vivid blue eyes and pale skin, she was the epitome of Irish girlhood. The mother superior had already explained to him that Colleen felt that she had a vocation. Time might prove otherwise, but for the present, the girl's mind appeared to be set firmly on that course.

Of course, he tried to talk Colleen out of it, and inwardly berated himself for not formally adopting her when she was small. He had offered this, but Colleen's mother, with a husband in view and not wanting to lose her baby, had refused. Harry was fond of Colleen, and had hoped one day to see her happily married, and to be able to act as benefactor to her own children.

'Look,' he said, persuasively, 'don't make up your mind yet. You know how fond you are of music. I'm more than willing to arrange things so you can go overseas and study some more under better teachers that you'll ever find here in Victoria. Then, perhaps, you can start up a school of your own. Times are changing, Colleen. Women are going out nursing, and teaching, and they can go a long way if they set their minds to it. You could be making a mistake by going into orders so young.'

'You must let me discover this for myself, father.'

'And what does your mother say, eh?'

He had not spoken directly to Colleen's mother for nigh on sixteen years, not since she had married.

'Every good Catholic mother hopes that she will give a child to the Church, father. Oh, don't look so cross. I know what I'm doing.'

'I wonder if you do.' He thought of the wild passions he had shared with her mother, and for a few moments was on the point of reminding Colleen that if things had been left to her mother, there would have been no long and expensive education at the best convent school Melbourne had to offer. Instead, he hugged Colleen affectionately.

'I haven't the legal right to tell you what to do, Colleen, more's the pity. You know that. But if you change your mind about the music, let me know.'

As he spoke, he knew that Colleen would not change her mind. There was already about her an air of apartness, of dedication.

This attended to, Harry found some other business to make this out-of-season journey to Melbourne worthwhile. Helena, like any other woman isolated from the city most of the year, found plenty to do, to such effect, that on their last night in Melbourne she confessed that she was quite worn out and happy to spend the evening reading whilst he dined at his club.

They were staying at a hotel, which annoyed Harry. In the old days, when he was single, he had always put up at his club, which offered far better accommodation and service than any Melbourne hotel, and nowadays, when the couple made their twice yearly descents upon the capital, they preferred to rent a furnished house.

As far as he was concerned, there was nothing right with the hotel. He hated eating his meals in public, food was inevitably cold if served in their room, he disliked the odd noises in the night, and he tended to look down his nose at other guests forced into this type of lodging. Helena kept her own counsel, but although she could find faults, she thought it restful not to be supervising a team of servants, which is what happened when they rented a house. As for Harry leaving her while he caught up on town and business gossip at his club, she could only look upon the chance to read under gaslight as a luxury. Garranbete was as modern and well-fitted as any Australian country house could be, but it lacked the convenience of town gas.

She could still chuckle over her amazement when she had first seen Garranbete. She had expected a small timber homestead, such as she had seen in pictures in magazine articles depicting Australian life. Instead, an imposing edifice, constructed of the basaltic stone called bluestone, had surprised her both by its solidarity and its size. Harry's builders had done their job well. This was a house to last for generations, and if the unfurnished rooms, littered with the numerous boxes and crates sent home from his travels, were not very welcoming to a new wife, his former homestead was still comfortable and did very well until the new house was fit for occupancy.

Harry was quite inordinately, almost ridiculously, proud of his new house. It wasn't as big as Robert's, he admitted, but the outlook was better, especially from the tower. Garranbete, for the new house had taken the name of the run, followed the practice of all the Western District mansions in having a tower added to the structure, reached, in this case, by a narrow set of stairs without a handrail. The purpose was not only that of fashion, for in this country, which could dry out dramatically after a few hot and windy days, bushfire was always a threat during summer. On the obviously dangerous days, a man would be installed on this look-out, to watch for the warning puff of smoke which could swell within minutes into a terrifying holocaust, destroying pasture, stock, fences, buildings and humans, without discrimination. Snobbery

being what it is, many Melbourne mer-
chants, safe on their suburban estates, added
towers to their own homes, thus placing
themselves on an equal footing (they hoped)
with the socially superior squatters.

Therefore, on the day following their
arrival at Garranbete, whilst Helena still
gazed about her in wonderment and with
some qualms as she faced the enormous job
of turning the new mansion into a home for
them both, Harry took her up to the tower,
scrambling nimbly up the steps himself, and
turning to help his hesitant bride upwards.

'Look at that,' he cried, proudly, with an
encompassing gesture. 'All Radford land.
Right to the mountains!'

In the distance, to the northwest, she
could discern a purple and serrated range,
and this being September, early spring here
in the Antipodes, the rolling land betwixt
was green and beautiful in the soft, clear
sunshine, darkened here and there by bush
which had escaped the clearing process,
splashed intermittently by patches of golden
wattle, and dotted inevitably by sheep in
their thousands.

'Near the hills is Dick's land. Robert's is to
the east, and all this about here is mine.
When we first came, it was all scrub and

forest. A wilderness. Look at it now.'

Then he turned towards the coastline, about four miles from Garranbete homestead, and sobered.

'Except that,' he amended, sourly.

Because, after a showery night, the air was so clear, she could see the white line of dunes holding the ocean at bay, and beyond that the blue sea spreading away to meet the sky, dappled by light grey cloud.

'Here,' he said, and handed her his expensive German field glasses. 'You can see the river behind the dunes with this. It flows along for a few miles on this side before turning off into the sea. And that bastard Eggert's house.'

'Harry,' she reproved him, as she always did when he let slip a violent word.

'All right. *Mr* Eggert's house, if you like,' he responded sulkily.

Eggert's presence on that land was a continuing sore spot with him. Helena had already heard about it, during their voyage to Australia, when he had spoken so much about the early days at Garranbete. In those times, he and his older brothers, well into manhood while he was still a lad, had slept with loaded guns within easy reach in case of attack by blacks. The blacks, of course, were almost gone now, through disease mostly, although there had been little wars of reprisal over stolen lubras and murdered shepherds, and one tragic incident when several aboriginal tribesmen had perished horribly after eating stolen sheep which had been smeared with an arsenical ointment to combat the skin disease called scab.

'Frank Stott told me this morning that Eggert's married,' he continued. Stott was the overseer, who, with Robert Radford, had managed the run during Harry's absence. 'Can't imagine who'd be stupid enough to marry Wesley Eggert. He's half off his head at the best of times, and when he's drunk he's right off it.'

Helena adjusted the glasses, and studied the Eggert farm, a collection of small buildings, grey in the distance. Then, lifting her eyes slightly, and holding her hair in place with her free hand, for a brisk breeze was rising, she found a dim shape out to sea.

'Harry. Is that an island?'

'Yes. Lady Julia Percy Island. Don't know who she was, but that's the name of it. I think it was Lady Julian Piercy – *P-i-e-r-c-y* – but it's been changed.'

'Well, it's no wonder you don't know whom she may have been.'

'The sealers used to land there to kill the seals, but when there weren't any left worth the taking, they stopped coming. There's a wrecked ship somewhere in the sandhills, Lena. Over a bit to your left. That's it. That's the spot. I saw it first, oh, about twenty-five years back. I was only a boy at the time. We were out looking for lost stock. The wood was dark, like mahogany, you know, a bit reddish, and the ship was high at the stern, like old pictures of galleons. A couple of weeks later I took my brothers back to the place, but there'd been a gale and the sand had covered it again. If it hadn't been that Sam the old shepherd had seen it too, they wouldn't have believed me. Then about fifteen years back, I saw it again. Same thing happened, though. It was covered up within the week, and I haven't seen it since. I'd like to look for it again, now I've more time, but it's on Eggert's land.'

'Couldn't you ask him if you can search? If the ship is hidden in the hummocks, surely it wouldn't matter very much to him. He doesn't use the sand for anything, surely.'

'Ask Eggert for anything? I'd as soon ask a dingo for favours. Come on, I've work to do.'

Talking about Eggert annoyed him, and

Helena began to understand the meaning of the old saying, a thorn in his side. That was what Eggert was to Harry Radford.

If Eggert irritated Harry, Helena had her own thorn in Ailsa, Robert's wife. Helena knew instantly, at their first meeting, that Ailsa resented her, and she was old enough, and experienced enough, to realise why, at least partly.

Until Helena had arrived, Ailsa had been undisputed *chatelaine* of the whole district. In the tiny local township of Wicklow, she was *the* Mrs Radford, mentioned in a somewhat hushed whisper, gazed upon by the womenfolk with envy and admiration, rather like an earl's wife back in England. Now there were two Mrs Radfords, and the newer one was a few years younger, better looking, and had rather more breeding than the other.

What Helena did not understand was that there was a little more to Ailsa's antipathy than straightforward jealousy. Ailsa was a born organiser who liked everything arranged to her own benefit. Harry had been that social asset, a personable, eligible bachelor, always available for dinners, dances, and the like. Ailsa also looked upon him as a pawn in her own little chess game of social advancement. Harry's clinging to his single state did not worry her: the Radfords were late marriers, as proved by both Richard and Robert. But when he did decide to wed, Ailsa hoped – no, planned – that it should be to a bride who would move the Radfords another step upwards on the ladder.

Instead, some weeks before the newlyweds actually arrived back in Victoria, she received a somewhat distressed letter from Blanche. Blanche was a person who always tried to think the best of everyone, and she was genuinely kind, but she had been startled, to say the least of it, when her brother-in-law had fixed his attentions upon Miss Clayton.

'Good connections, but in the distance, if you know what I mean, and *absolutely no money.* It is really the worst luck that she should have been home at this time. She lost her post – she is a governess – in London and had to return here until she found another. Rather handsome, was engaged before, to a widower in the Indian Army, but he died out there. Harry, poor man, is quite head over heels. At least, in that affair with the O'Halloran girl all those years ago, he did have the sense not to marry her. As much as I try, Ailsa, I cannot help feeling that Miss Clayton has *seized an opportunity.*'

These were very strong views indeed, from someone as mild as Blanche. Ailsa, naturally, could not know that to a degree Blanche's view was coloured by the remembrance of many little off-hand snubs delivered by those county people with whom the poverty-stricken Claytons were on level terms, socially, if not financially.

Ailsa lost no time in telling Helena that *their* house was larger, and not only larger than Rowland's (she always called Harry by his correct name), but also Richard's. She dropped the names of prominent persons she knew in Melbourne with all the subtlety of a dray unloading bricks, and talked about money.

Helena found this aspect of Victorian life most trying. People discussed financial matters as hunting devotees in her father's circle had talked about horses. It was understandable that the flockmasters, like Harry and Robert Radford, should have a never-ending interest in wool prices, but the way in which Ailsa and her friends constantly pushed pounds, shillings and pence, or even better guineas, at one another, astonished Helena.

A dress was not merely a pleasing colour. The material cost so much a yard, and then the dressmaker added braid and lace at some exorbitant price ('French, of course') and put in her own bill, too high, but worth every penny. Someone who paid fifty pounds for a piece of carpet moved ahead of her rival who had innocently expended a mere forty-eight pounds ten shillings, and was stupid enough to mention it to her best friend.

Ailsa was a true product of the Melbourne which had been bloated by riches pouring in from the goldfields. Helena's family had always been in straitened circumstances, as long as she could recollect, and the need for economy was discussed within the closest domestic circle, but whether Helena had spent two-pence a yard for ribbon, or ten shillings, she would not have mentioned it past her front door. To do so was in bad taste. Neither, in the wealthy and aristocratic household where she had been employed as governess, was the sordid subject of money bandied about. The family simply possessed it, and had for a long time.

Yet, Ailsa had many good qualities. She was a good housekeeper, a mother who deeply cared that her children were properly educated and kept in good health, and she simply flew to the aid of those in need. The Irish tenant farmers who formed the close-knit community which centred about Wicklow, that tiny township huddled at the foot of a long extinct volcano to the east of Garranbete, had many tales of how Mrs Radford – Mrs Robert, that was – had never hesitated to go into a poor shack to take care of sick children, or a mother forced to her bed.

At first, they reserved their opinion of Mrs Harry. She seemed a bit quiet, perhaps, or was she just stuck up?

Still, over three years, it was noticed that Mrs Harry had her own way of doing things, and it was even observed by one of the wiseheads at the Rose of Tralee that when Mrs Harry did a body a good turn, she did not leave the recipient feeling under a life-long obligation. She did things because she was a good Christian lady, not because she wanted to make a show, and Con O'Brien, new owner and licensee of the public house, agreed.

It was a pity she had not had kids yet, added another bar pundit. A disappointment to Mr Harry, it must be.

Bar gossip was right. Helena and Harry

were happy, a complete antithesis of the old saying about marrying in haste and repenting at leisure, but their lack of issue was a continuing worry to Helena. Harry tried to cheer her up when she brooded about this, by saying that he had dozens of strapping nephews, both through his brothers, and his sisters over in Tasmania, but she sensed that he was being kind and that he was too fond of her to hurt her feelings.

To Harry, the most painful part about it was that Helena had become pregnant immediately after their marriage. Then, following a fall during a patch of rough weather on the voyage out, she had, as the delicate expressed it, 'lost her hopes'. The ship's doctor had assured Harry that no permanent harm had been done, but the months passed and Helena did not again conceive. She consulted doctors in Melbourne, who told her that she was a perfectly healthy woman, though on the last occasion, one added the rider that she was now in her thirties, and that sometimes women past their twenties found it more difficult to become pregnant. Being historically minded, he mentioned the well-known cases of Catherine of Aragon and

Empress Josephine of France, who had found themselves past childbearing at a comparatively early age. He did not bother to point out that although these ladies had been unable to oblige their lords when they reached their thirties, they had in fact both borne children earlier in life. Helena did not have that satisfaction.

Still, she did not waste time wallowing in self pity. The little ache was always there, but there was plenty to occupy her days. First of all, the big bluestone house had to be set to rights, and this was a task which seemed without end. Then, new servants had to be trained into her ways, and there was entertaining and visiting, and picnic races, and trips to Melbourne, over and above the inevitable cycle of sheep-raising. It now fell to her, as mistress of the establishment, to keep an eye on the kitchen garden, the poultry, and the making of jams and preserves from the fruit produced by the orchard. It was also her duty to take an interest in any very young teen-aged boys who were employed on the run, to see that their health did not suffer from the very long hours they worked, and that they somehow found time to acquire a little education. For the squatter's wife, daily routine resembled more closely that of a wealthy English countrywoman in a previous century than the life of the contemporary well-to-do back Home.

Thus, at the end of three years from the time she had first arrived at Garranbete, Helena could think of herself as a settled wife, past her first mistakes in household supervision, and turning the energies which could have been given to child-bearing towards creating a landscaped garden which already promised to become a showplace, and imprinting her natural good taste throughout their home.

Part of her time during this September trip to Melbourne had been spent in commissioning an artist to undertake a series of pictures of the countryside about Garranbete. Helena could not help feeling pleased about this scheme. It would, she knew, annoy Ailsa very much, for Ailsa had never thought of having her great house copied on to canvas. He was an excellent artist, too, not one of your amateur daubers, but a man who could have made a living in London or Europe.

Ailsa, as it turned out, would have far more to be annoyed about than Helena's hiring of an artist. And Ailsa would not only be annoyed. She would be prodded into a jealous fury which would have the most disastrous consequences for her brother-in-law's wife.

Six

When Harry returned from his club at about eleven o'clock, Helena, glancing up from her novel, thought at first that her husband was tipsy. He certainly had a glow about him, and a beaming grin on his face. But, although he smelt of good brandy and cigars as he leant over her and kissed her, he was quite sober.

'Oh, Lena,' he exclaimed, bursting into a laugh, 'you'll never guess what's happened in a million years.'

And he sat down with a bounce on the bed, and began to laugh some more.

'Well,' she commented, smiling too, 'it must be very funny. You'd best tell me so that I can share in the joke.' As she spoke, she drew his arm about her, for she never tired of feeling his strong body against hers.

'Try. Guess.'

89

'Oh, Harry, how can I? You haven't given me even a hint as to what all this is about.'

'Well,' he said, slowly and mysteriously, his eyes dancing with mischief, 'what has all Melbourne been talking about this past week?'

Helena had spent much of their stay bustling about her own business, find that artist, executing a few small commissions for Mrs Stott, the overseer's wife, and discussing with a prominent botanist which imported plants could best be acclimatised in her garden. Because of the suddenness of their journey, they had made few social arrangements, and had spent their evenings together, either reading quietly here at the hotel, or at theatres. Still, they would have had to have been quite impervious to the rest of the world not to have heard, and discussed, the big event of the year.

Or was it the big event of the decade, or perhaps of the century?

His Royal Highness, Prince Alfred Arthur George, Duke of Edinburgh, Earl of Ulster, Duke of Kent, and Prince of Saxe-Coburg-Gotha, was on his way to the Australian colonies during the course of his world tour as commander of the *Galatea*.

The news was a little garbled, and there

could only be educated guesses as to when the distinguished visitor would arrive, to be the first member of Britain's ruling house to step on Australian soil. Overseas news still travelled slowly by ship, and even the few days saved by telegraphing important items overland from Adelaide, the port of call before Melbourne, was considered an enormous advance. In 1867, the South Australians were already contemplating the construction of an overland telegraph from Adelaide to Port Darwin, on Australia's far northern coastline, to link with an underseas cable from India, but until this became reality, the Australian colonies had to remain at the mercy of ship-borne news.

'Oh, you mean Prince Alfred's visit,' said Helena, now. 'I know. We've been invited as guests to a reception.'

She had expected this. Harry had been a member of Parliament, was a member of the exclusive Melbourne Club, a great land-owner, a leading wool producer, and generally a man of standing in Victoria.

'More than that. I was approached tonight – Lena, Ailsa's never going to forgive us for this. We're going to entertain Prince Alfred at Garranbete. Oh, just for a luncheon, while he's touring the Western District. The

Austins at Winchelsea 'll have him overnight, and so will Hopkins at Warnambool, but dammit, Lena, imagine us entertaining one of Queen Victoria's sons?'

Helena's first feeling was not of elation, but of dark despair, the frequent reaction of the ordinary mortal when faced with the prospect of entertaining the exalted. Her mind raced over her garden, not yet properly grown, counted out the silver, looked at her chinaware, and examined her linen, all in the space of ten seconds, also taking in the shortcomings of her cook as a side issue.

'Oh, no,' she gasped.

'What do you mean, oh no? Lena, it's the greatest honour we could have. Lor', when I was a boy, trailing after my big brothers, and mucking in after the sheep, I certainly never expected anything like this. Prince Alfred at our house. Y'know, when I was in London, I saw the Prince of Wales from a distance, twice, and I thought I was lucky.'

'It's just … oh, Harry, do you think we can cope?'

'Cope? What do you mean, cope? Of course we can.' He grabbed both her hands. 'And it's because of you, Lena. That's what – well, no names can be mentioned yet – told me. Government House thought of Robert first, because their house is bigger and quite famous, but they're scared Ailsa might say something out of place.'

Helena could well imagine that. Ailsa was just as likely as not to enquire of His Royal Highness how much his coat had cost.

When the Radfords breakfasted the next morning, they were still both in a state of euphoria. Not a word was to be divulged to anyone at this time, and the arrangement had to be confirmed by letter, but anyone looking at them must have guessed that something remarkable had occurred.

Still, Harry did not much like eating his breakfast in full view of other persons, and he made his usual remark to this effect.

Helena kept her smile to herself, and thought what a dear, darling person he was. On the surface, the powerful wool baron, sometimes a little unscrupulous (she had no idea of the things which had been written in the popular press about the Radfords and other graziers as they bought up land meant for small farmers), but with those funny little quirks which constantly endeared him to her. His fad about the island, for instance, his hatred of hotels (well, Melbourne's hotels were not *quite* the best in the world) and his childish triumph over being asked to entertain the Prince.

'And look at that fellow over there,' continued Harry, cutting into a sausage like a surgeon performing a post mortem. 'A Yankee stove salesman. I tell you, Lena, that's hotels for you. All sorts.'

'It does make life interesting,' she murmured, but she glanced towards the offending Yankee salesman. Her mind was still dwelling on the shortcomings of her kitchen arrangements, and she wondered whether it would be worth installing another range to cope with the situation. Then common sense intruded. They had managed quite well last Easter Saturday, when they had entertained a hundred people after the local race meeting.

The salesman was a man of just over medium height, of sinewy rather than muscular build, with ginger-red hair cut fairly short, and a well trimmed full beard to match. The very cold blue eyes met hers in open speculation for a moment, stripping her down and challenging her to do something about it. It shocked her. He had, at first glance, appeared so inoffensive in his sombre clothes, not at all Yankee flashy as one would have expected of an American travelling salesman.

'He's got mange on his right jaw,' said Harry, in a voice just above a murmur. 'He should grow his beard a bit bushier to hide it.'

Helena did not wish to look in the redheaded man's direction again, but as they walked out of the dining-room, to leave the hotel for the railway station, she managed a quick peek and saw the white patch of scar tissue amidst the whiskers.

'How did you know the man was a stove salesman?' she asked, as they crossed the lobby. She had detested the American on sight. He had stared at her as if she were a street girl. But, although Helena was insulted, she was also aware of a deep sense of excitement too. Oh, chase the thought away. It was not worthy of her. It made her feel dirty.

'Heard him talking last night when I came in. Typical big-mouthed Yankee. Talking about how everything is better in the States. Don't know why he didn't stay there. Name's Doherty. Sam Doherty. Hope he doesn't come out Garranbete way trying to sell us a stove.'

The man Doherty came out of the hotel as they climbed into their cab, and once again,

Helena felt him looking at her. His eyes could see into her. She was sure of it, and pulled her jacket closer about her. And then she began to be frightened. Surely he could not know? How could he? He was an Irish American, bent on selling patent stoves in Victoria. Yankee salesmen had never touched her English world. She had trained herself to forget about it. It was in the past. Only three people knew, and she was one of them.

Helena grabbed Harry's arm, and as she felt the strength of it, her sudden fears began to subside, and she relaxed as they were borne swiftly towards the railway station.

The man was merely an insolent lecher. It was all over and done with years ago, and it was only her conscience which made her feel this awful trepidation. Everything had worked out for the best. In spite of Helena's assurances to her inner self, the unease – and the guilt – had returned to stay.

Sam Doherty, the cheeky salesman, smiled to himself as he watched Mrs Radford being handed into the cab by her attentive husband. He had not the slightest idea whom she might be, and did not care much, but he was pleased at her reaction to his bold gaze. Major Stephen Doyle had been known for his austere, almost monk-like style of existence, and he knew that disguising oneself was more than a matter of changing one's style of facial growth or dyeing one's hair. Dye was a messy and tricky affair, especially with red hair, which had, he was told, the disconcerting habit of turning any shade but black when one made the attempt. He had compromised by the application of a mildly bleaching solution which toned his fiery locks down to ginger.

That same morning, as the train bearing the Radfords on the first leg of their homeward journey chugged up the escarpment towards Ballarat, the erstwhile Major Doyle, soldier of the Union, and present Fenian, had an appointment. At eleven o'clock he was received by the Honourable Member for Ballarat, a certain Peter Lalor.

Peter Lalor was then forty years of age, a tall, solid, greying, dignified man, who nowadays did not seem the person to have led a wild rebellion of gold miners against the Victorian government back in 1854. However, there was a perpetual reminder of his involvement in the notorious Eureka incident at Ballarat in the left sleeve of his coat, which was empty, and pinned up neatly. He had come to Australia from his native Ireland as a civil engineer in 1852, but had gone to the goldfields, eventually finding himself caught up in the wild revolt of miners which was nominally over the unfair licensing system, but which had strong undertones of Irish against the Saxon. After the short, disastrous pitched fight, he had gone into hiding with a price on his head and a bullet-shattered left arm which was later amputated at the shoulder. Several months later, he came out of hiding, was tried, and declared not guilty by a sympathetic jury.

The participants in the rebellion all considered that they had brought about sweeping democratic changes in Victoria's administration. This was an illusion which made it all seem worthwhile, for even as they plotted their ineffectual revolution, the new constitution giving Victoria a parliament and self rule was on its way by sea from Westminster.

Peter Lalor stood for Parliament, the lower House of Assembly, and was elected, and had represented Ballarat ever since. He was no illiterate bog Irishman. He was university educated, with the practical streak of an engineer, and soon shocked his wilder supporters by declaring against universal (male) franchise, which, however, was carried. Still, in spite of being a reactionary who believed in a property qualification for a voting right, he pleased his electorate, and settled down to a long, somewhat undistinguished career in politics. The dashing young man who led a rebellion, was defeated, and so romantically concealed for months by a devoted fiancée, became, as years passed, a rather stodgy pillar of the establishment.

The visitor wasted no time in coming to the point of this call on Mr Lalor. He had, he said, fought for the Union during the late American war, and had been a comrade-in-arms alongside one of Mr Lalor's brothers.

'And a splendid foighter he was,' declared Sam Doherty, emphasising an Irishness not usually apparent in his speech.

Lalor regarded him steadily for some seconds.

'My brothers have all been fighters,' he said. 'I lost five, you know, in the American war. Three on one side, two on the other. I'm inclined to think that fighting doesn't achieve much except women's tears, Mr Doherty.'

Major Doyle, who had never known a

soldier called Lalor, but who had done his homework, began to realise that his assumption that the hero of Eureka would help him was astray. He had based his hopes upon the fierce hatred of Fintan, one of Peter's sixteen brothers, for anything British, and upon Peter's legendary reputation. He had overlooked the strong feeling for law and order which also ran through some of the Lalor blood. Lalor the father of that huge tribe had been a member of parliament, as was yet another of Peter's brothers who sat in the House of Commons.

So, there it was, a pleasant enough meeting, but one which ended with a handshake and a word of thanks for taking the bother to tell him about his brother's courageous end on an American battlefield.

Seven

During October, preparations for the Prince's visit to the eastern states of Australia progressed, although, of course, there could be no firm time-table. One definite plan was that a tour of Victoria's fertile Western District should culminate in a stay at Ballarat, the famous gold rush city, which stood on high land forming the northern boundary of the volcanic plains.

Throughout the country, there were being erected triumphal arches by the dozen. (Colonial Australia was very fond of triumphal arches, especially for newly arrived Governors, who, as often as not, would later slink back to Britain covered with public contempt.) These, according to local financial resources, ranged from humble efforts decorated with leafy boughs to sophisticated marvels featuring electric lights. A brisk trade in small Union Jacks was already reported by many stores, and school children everywhere were being drilled into the proper procedure of singing 'God Save the Queen'. In South Australia, they added the local anthem, 'The Song of Australia'.

In Melbourne, a doctor who had made a fortune by dealing in mail order medicine, was already planning a tour-de-force to encourage the drinking of local wine. His vision was quite splendid. A vast feast for the poor, in honour of His Royal Highness's visit, was to be lubricated by wine from picturesque fountains erected on one of the city's public reserves. Not only did he plan it, but he managed to arouse such enthusiasm for the idea amidst Melbourne's prosperous tradespeople, that before long literally thousands of pounds worth of food was being offered for the occasion. Society ladies undertook to arrange the whole thing, and for some baffling reason, they saw the occasion coloured by delicacy and refinement. Even the most unworldly of them should have been aware that Melbourne's lower orders included some of the worst ruffians in the Southern Hemisphere, the flotsam left behind by the great wave of gold seekers in the previous decade.

At Garranbete, Helena began preparations, but with dates not settled, it was hard to do anything definite. It was known that the visitor would spend a short time with a family called Austin, not because of the magnificence of their homestead, but because Mr Austin had managed to acclimatise rabbits on his property, and it was well known that Prince Alfred revelled in shooting and hunting. In the past, others had tried to stock their paddocks with wild rabbits for the sake of sport, but without success. The ordinary grey European rabbit did not care for Australian conditions. However, Mr Austin's consignment had included a few brown domestic rabbits, and the mutation worked. Their rusty-grey progeny bounded from those first burrows to set up homes of their own, and start a major ecological tragedy.

After leaving the Austins and their rabbits, it was intended that Prince Alfred should travel westwards, staying at the grandest of the sheep lords' homes, and taking in a kangaroo shoot on the way. Harry tried to think of something to match the rabbits and kangaroo shoot. He rather envied the Austins their lucky foresight, for, like most other graziers, he had no idea of what had been unleashed when those few travelworn rabbits had been let loose.

He toyed with the notion of another kangaroo shoot, but dismissed it for two reasons. One was that the novelty would have worn off, and the other was that he could see nothing attractive in cooping up a number of wild animals in an enclosure to be released to give someone a few easy shots. In the early days, he had enjoyed kangaroo hunting on horseback, with good dogs streaking along ahead after the big marsupials. Nowadays, he kept a policy of live and let live as far as the pouched animals were concerned. If they became too numerous, he hired a professional shooter to reduce their ranks. Secretly, he rather liked to come upon a small group of them unexpectedly. It reminded him of the wild, rough days of his boyhood, when danger and hardship had been balanced by the sheer freedom of life in a vast, unfenced land where the wildfowl gathered thick on the marshes and a hillock climbed could spread before him a stretch of country never before seen by a white man's eyes.

Helena decided that a picnic style luncheon on a pleasant clearing near the river would be best. His Royal Highness was to be treated to so much pomp, she reasoned, that a little informality might be welcome. The spot she had in mind was always well shaded, even on the hottest day, and if Harry could keep the sheep away from it for a few weeks, the grass would grow, and could even be mown before the great occasion. If, by some mischance, the weather was unkind, there was sufficient room both inside the house and under the wide veranda, if the french doors were opened, for a very large party.

Harry agreed, and although they still did

not know the exact date for this event, practical steps were taken. The chosen place near the river was fenced off, and serious consideration given to the wine supplies, for although a picnic was planned, it was not going to be typically Australian with indifferent food washed down by scalding smoke-flavoured tea.

Harry examined his wine cellar, and consulted the lists forwarded to him regularly by a Melbourne merchant. He wanted, if possible, to provide wine grown in Victoria, but could he take the risk? He thought of the royal palate being shrivelled by liquid too acid or too sweet, and decided ultimately to have both imported and local wines available.

These discussions took place privately between Harry and Helena, for both had a marked reluctance to tell Ailsa about the arrangement. When Robert asked why the area near the river had been fenced off, Harry muttered something about the bank wearing away badly in that spot.

On the last day of October, some Adelaide men out fishing in the early morning were astounded to see the steam frigate *Galatea* riding at anchor in Holdfast Bay, six miles from the South Australian capital. The vessel had come in quietly during the night, unobserved by those who had been watching eagerly for the past fortnight. Within the hour, news was travelling to Melbourne, and on to Sydney, via the electric telegraph. Prince Alfred was in Australia, and dates could be fixed, and arrangements, which had been going forward steadily, solidified.

Stephen Doyle bought an early edition as soon as the newspapers hit the Melbourne streets. So, the *Galatea* was lying off Adelaide. The rumour which had brought him, prematurely, to Melbourne was correct. It was here, in Victoria, amidst the unthinking and sentimental patriotism of these colonials, that he would have his opportunity. Yet, Doyle had doubts about Melbourne itself.

He tried to think ahead to the Prince's arrival. The *Galatea* would have to pass through the Heads, having taken on a pilot from the village of Queenscliff on the western pincer. Then it would steam the fifty or sixty miles up across Port Phillip Bay to the capital, but it was unlikely that the warship could come in sufficiently close to the shore at any one point to allow a marksman a clear shot.

For Doyle, Melbourne, now frantically

finishing off triumphal arches and erecting wooden stands to give the citizens a better look at the visitor, had a serious drawback. This city swanked incessantly about its remarkable growth from a riverside village back in 1836 to its present half a million inhabitants (which made it the largest city in Australia) and even referred to itself as Marvellous Melbourne. However, despite the bragging and undoubted progress, it would have been hard to find any building more than three stories in height. Land was plentiful and cheap. If one wanted to expand, one did so sideways, not upwards. To find an elevated and unremarked place from which to take careful aim and fire that fatal shot was going to be difficult with every vantage point at a premium.

Over the past weeks, the erstwhile Union officer had been able to create, in a piecemeal way, a fair idea of what routes the young Prince would be likely to follow during his stay in Victoria. The Royal Reception Committee received endless publicity, not always very kind, in the columns of the daily press, and by the time that Prince Alfred arrived in Adelaide, Stephen Doyle knew just where he would be going whilst in Victoria.

By now, Doyle was becoming resigned to the knowledge that he would probably have to carry out his mission single-handed. Like the United States, Australia was a stronghold of expatriate Irishmen, but here the Fenian movement lacked the vigour it possessed in the American republic, where England was still regarded with some suspicion and dislike. As Sam Doherty, Major Doyle was already a member of Melbourne's Hibernian Club, and he had soon realised that Victoria's Irish were reasonably contented with their lot under the British flag. On those two fateful anniversaries, July 12th, when 'King Billy' had trounced the Jacobites at Boyne Water, and the 18th December, also commemorating an episode the best part of two centuries since, orange and green sometimes came to blows, but usually both factions had better things to do.

True, many of the convicts transported to Australia in the old days had borne Irish names, but many of them were Londoners of several generations, and burglars rather than daring patriots. At any rate, by 1867, the surviving 'old hands' in the eastern Australian colonies were either too old, too well settled, or too drink sodden to engage in any conspiracy.

Before long, Stephen Doyle began to understand the differences between an Irishman in Australia and one in America. A most important item was distance. It cost more to travel to Australia, and so the majority of Australian immigrants were not quite so down-trodden or poverty-stricken as those who sailed across the Atlantic. Also, because it was harder to persuade people to migrate to Australia, laws governing the state of the ships used were stricter. The notorious coffin ships used on the Atlantic run to shift Ireland's starving peasants would not have passed a first inspection if intended for Australia.

In Australia, a newly landed Irish immigrant often found himself heading 'up country' looking for work, instead of being huddled into a close-knit American slum community which fed labour into mills and factories as steaming and evil as any in the Old World. Thus, Irish resentments were more apt to be dispersed, and the Irishman often had an almost immediate sense of having bettered himself rather than having moved from one wretched situation into another.

Whatever the causes, Melbourne's Irishmen, although they still talked long and noisily about their wrongs, were more given to speech than action. They remembered Vinegar Hill, they hated Oliver Cromwell, (or admired him, according to which club they patronised) and they were all familiar with the agonies of the Great Famine, but where were the men who, if given a similar chance, would have marched with John O'Neill into British Canada from the United States, and whipped a detachment of Canadian volunteers? Had nothing happened to just one of these Melbourne Irish to hone his hatreds into the fine, single purpose which had driven Stephen Doyle across the world?

Why had he not accomplished his design back in Marseilles? Why had chance intervened, to send him fleeing through the back alleys, leaving behind a dead woman and the one object he had valued above all else? The one treasure of the family of which he was now the only surviving member?

When he was beset by doubts, he drew out that last memory of his twin sister, in much the way a drunkard would take a bottle of spirits from a hiding place. Always, it acted in the same fashion, turning his heart back into steel, firming his resolution, convincing him that his purpose was a part of destiny.

Sheelagh had died during that dreadful second winter in New York. Her poor slight body, already weakened by her privations as a child during the years of the potato blight, had yielded readily to the influenza sweeping through the tenements. Her twin had laid next to her all during that last night, trying to warm her body with his, attempting to hold her so that air could reach down into her tortured lungs.

At dawn she had been able to catch her breath.

'You're so good, Stephen,' she had whispered. 'So good.'

Five minutes later she was dead, still holding their mother's rosary in her fingers. He had sat down then, and wept and cursed, and begged for Heaven's vengeance upon those whose indifference had placed his family in a trail of graves across Ireland's famished soil and beneath the Atlantic waters.

Eight

When Ailsa Radford learned that the Prince would by-pass her own home and be entertained at the smaller, less impressive Garranbete homestead, she flew into a jealous rage. She had never cared for Helena, and had frequently remarked to her husband in private that *there* was someone who had landed on her feet. One of those poverty-stricken, genteel Englishwomen who looked down upon colonials, but did not hesitate to marry one if he had money, that's what she was.

Helena and Harry, dreading the thought of telling her, had foolishly put it off until Ailsa read about the Prince's proposed itinerary. Robert took it cheerfully enough. He would have all the pleasure, he said, and none of the expense, of meeting His Royal Highness after someone else had done all the work. His wife, on the other hand, made it very clear to her brother-in-law and Helena that she would never forgive this slight, and she was quite convinced that

Harry had used his influence as a former member of the Legislative Council to gain this honour.

It was fortunate that shearing time coincided with the bombshell, for it kept both households so busy that Ailsa and Helena did not have time to build up the feud which had been forced into the open.

As well as planning for the Garranbete picnic, there was a trip to Melbourne to be fitted in between the drilling of servants, the organising of supplies, and constant prayers that the weather would be kind on The Day. A gilt-edged invitation to the Grand State Ball in Melbourne had duly arrived, and fortunately, its twin was delivered to Mr and Mrs Robert Radford.

Helena looked through her ample wardrobe in despair. Everything therein suddenly seemed quite old-fashioned and countrified. She needed a new ball gown, or perhaps two, and something suitable to wear on The Day. Harry assured her that he had managed perfectly well through shearing time before his marriage, and sent her off to Ballarat, the nearest large town, to visit her dressmaker. There was, of course, a woman at Wicklow who could do passable alterations and run up cotton dresses for summer days at home, but her style had not moved much past the provincial Irish town where she had been born.

So Helena put in an arduous day travelling by coach to Ballarat, accompanied by her personal maid, Miss McPherson, who was Scots and reliable.

The inhabitants considered that Ballarat was vastly superior to Melbourne, and in some ways they were right. The inland city had the advantage of having started off rich. Once it passed the tent stage, it had been able to build in the manner suitable to a town which had sprung up on one of the richest alluvial goldfields the world has ever known.

Its main street was much grander than any in Melbourne, and not only was it the centre of a rich gold mining area, but also provided the hub of a district where the squatters had thrived exceedingly. Its main hotel had a better reputation than any in the capital, and generally, it was hard to credit that less than twenty years since, there had been no elegant buildings embellished with ornate iron lacework, but only sheep, which certainly had no idea that the grass they nibbled had gold dust clinging to its roots.

Helena had something else on her mind

besides new dresses. The idea had been implanted some weeks earlier when she had overheard two of the servants talking about the illness of a third.

'She wants to do what me mother did,' said one, scornfully, as she polished an elaborate side table which had been amongst the many crate loads of furniture Harry Radford had purchased in Europe. 'You'd think the cove what made this did it on purpose to make it 'ard for us women,' she added, disgustedly, as she wiped about a bunch of grapes carved into the wood.

'Well, what did yer mother do?' demanded the other.

'Went to the Chinese 'erbalist. Fix anythin', they can. Fixed me mum up in no time. She was carryin' all this water, y'see. Took this stuff Num Soong sold 'er, and she was right in two shakes. She'd written to Dr Smith up in Melbourne, but 'is stuff didn't do no good.'

'You mean Mr Num what's got that funny little place off Sturt Street up in Ballarat? Near the turn off to Bakery Hill?'

Helena passed by without giving any sign that she had been listening, but almost immediately she began turning over in her mind Mr Num's name and address. Since she had lived in Australia, she had heard several tales of the allegedly remarkable cures brought about by recourse to Chinese herbalists, and like many others, she had the idea that the Orient was somehow both wiser and cleverer than the West.

At first, she was diffident about going to a herbalist. It smacked of witchcraft, the sort of village superstition her clergyman father had derided, and yet, was it not a fact that many of the simples prepared from plants were now being proved scientifically sound? What harm could there be in trying? Her sense of dignity and social position fought against her desire to snatch at any remedy which could cure her continuing childlessness, but when she reached Ballarat, her mind was made up.

Miss McPherson had a married sister living in Ballarat, and in the morning, Helena told her that she would not be required until early afternoon, when Helena would need assistance in changing to make one or two brief social calls.

Stephen Doyle had his own reasons for being in Ballarat. As Sam Doherty, he was energetically gaining customers for the stove company, for this part of his Australian mission was genuine. He was not a rich man, and the funds provided by his Fenian supporters back in the States were hardly sufficient for the barest day to day needs.

He had another, more sinister, purpose in choosing Ballarat as his latest venue. He had received a name, in a round-about-way, through casual conversation with a rising young Irish-bred politician back in Melbourne's Hibernian Club. This ambitious young upstart was no Fenian. He talked a lot about Ireland's wrongs to secure the votes of his Catholic constituents, but in the long run, he had his eye on the Premiership and a possible knighthood. He had, Major Doyle thought, a sneaking sympathy for the Fenian movement, but he could not afford to offend the priests of his church, who had never supported John O'Mahoney's American based secret society.

However, the politician did drop a name, that of a man with a brother active in one of the Fenian cadres. This man had himself been involved in the Ballarat troubles back in 1854, when so many of those who had made their pathetic attempt at revolution against the British flag had been Irish. Doyle, who was prepared to undertake the assassination of Prince Alfred singlehanded, was coming to realise that if he were to escape the country afterwards, he would need assistance.

Australia had a serious drawback. There were not enough people. In an old world seaport like Marseilles, with its large drifting population and its tightpacked old town, escape had been easy. There, he was just another stranger, but Australians, he had observed, all seemed to have a village type mentality. They were inquisitive about strangers, and news could spread across the empty land with astonishing speed. There were remote areas where the settlers helped bushrangers evade the law, but they were usually related to the bandits, or well paid for their trouble.

Captain Doyle wanted to escape afterwards. No one had ever questioned his courage under fire, but he had never been the sort to leap out into full view of the enemy and shake his fist. Assassination, he thought, was too often turned into an exercise of exhibitionism. Take the murder of Abraham Lincoln. John Wilkes Booth could have shot the President in a less public venue, and escaped to live to a ripe old age.

Stephen Doyle saw the English Prince's death as a catalyst, unleashing revolutionary forces right throughout the Empire, bringing about the downfall of the hated Saxon, and he wanted to be witness to these events.

He was unaware that this dream was as mad and muddled as that of the late John Wilkes Booth.

Ballarat, warm and prosperous in this November of 1867, was in a fair frenzy of preparation. Its welcoming arch would, when completed, be the largest in Australia, and workmen were frantically completing the Alfred Hall, to accommodate the grand balls, interminable speeches and florid banquets which would mark the royal visit. Every woman in Ballarat was brightening up her wardrobe according to her means, all the school children were being drilled, and the local gas company was turning itself inside out to provide illuminations.

Over in the Chinese quarter, a huge and traditional dragon was being constructed, and Chinese legs were being trained into the art of providing locomotion for the monster. At the same time, Chinese tailors stitched energetically to create gorgeous costumes to be worn in their part of the procession, costumes incidentally which would have placed the low-born Chinese of Ballarat into prison back in the Flowery Kingdom, for being so impudent as to move above their station in life. Yes, this was indeed to be Ballarat's most golden moment.

As Helena Radford allowed herself to be fitted – her figure was good and well-proportioned, and the dressmaker had been able to do quite an amount of the preliminary work on the gowns – Stephen Doyle paid a visit. His object was to sound out a man whom he hoped would assist in his escape from Victoria, and perhaps provide some sort of diversion to allow him his chance to shoot Prince Alfred.

His disappointment was to be bitter indeed, and yet, not without compensation, for, from this encounter, he received information which inspired him, finally, to firm his plans.

The man he wished to see was a helpless cripple, confined to his bed, reduced to a wreck by a mine cave-in about six months previously. So much for a politician's friendship, thought Doyle angrily, as he stood awkwardly at the foot of the man's bed.

'Sit down, sit down, Mr Doherty.' Will Joyce had all the Irishman's love of talk. 'I don't know ye, but I'm glad to see ye, all the same. Glad to see anyone these days.'

'I'm sorry about your accident.'

'Ah, who'd have thought Battling Will Joyce'd come to this. I'm lucky though. Maggie, that's me daughter, 's a good girl. She looks after me like a king. Now, ye've brought news of the Old Country, I take it.'

'In a way. I knew your brother Tom, God rest his soul.'

'Tom? Ye've the wrong brother, boy. Tom's here in Ballarat, fightin' fit, and drinkin' twice as much as any normal man. Ye must mean Paddy. Always was hotheaded, was Paddy.'

Damn, thought Doyle. That fool at the Hibernian Club mixed up the names. Now, the sharp dark eyes regarded him suspiciously.

'Ye don't know any of my brothers, not any of the whole seven of 'em. Now, what's ye're business. Out with it.'

'I'm sorry,' replied Doyle, thinking quickly. 'You're too smart to be fooled with tales about your brothers, though the one who was killed attacking Clerkenwell Gaol was a true hero, fit to fight alongside Finn MacCumhaill himself.'

He had deliberately introduced the name of the Irish mythological hero, gambling that his host would associate it with the word Fenian. A flash of understanding rewarded his perspicacity.

'Ah.' The cripple shifted himself painfully on his pillows. 'That's an ancient name. As old as *fianna*. Soldiers in the old tongue. Well, lad, me days are done, as ye can see. Tom's not interested. He didn't hold with what Paddy was doing. He's one of those who puts his faith in the House of Commons giving Home Rule back to Ireland. Talk, talk, talk, and nothing done, even while the children are starving to death in the cabins.'

'I'm counting heads,' said Doyle. 'There's no money to be had for the cause in Ireland. I came to Australia because I thought...' He was still picking his way carefully. 'But it's as you say, talk, talk, talk, and precious little doing. The trouble is, when a man gets a full belly, he forgets.'

'Not all,' said the other, and then laughed croakily. 'And why should I let you coax me into talking treason?'

'*I* don't talk treason. I'm an American citizen. During your so-called revolution here in Ballarat, no-one dared touch Americans, even though they were in it up to their necks.'

'When Paddy was killed, blown to bits by their own bomb they were, there was another fine man right at his side who has connections here in Victoria. His brother came to see me, and we held a wake befitting Brian Borugh himself, right here in this very room.' Joyce sighed deeply, his eyes moist. 'When Paddy was no more than eight years old, I took him to the very spot where King Brian died, at Clontarf, just outside Dublin, and he said, bless his dear soul, looking up at me with those big dark eyes of his, "When I grow up, I'm going to be a hero like King Brian." And he was.'

He moved again on his pillows, and produced a bottle of whisky from a hiding place amidst the blankets.

'Tom brings me this. Maggie'd kill him if she found out. Slip out into the kitchen while she's in the yard, lad, and fetch two glasses.'

'And this man you mentioned,' asked Doyle some minutes later as he sipped the potent and not very good spirit, 'does he live in Ballarat, now?'

What a lot of talking to get to so very little.

'Oh, no, lad. Down by the coast, he lives. A lot of Irishmen farm thereabouts, potatoes mostly, and working for the big squatters. Place called Wicklow, and a fine name that is. Saw in the paper yesterday that this Prince Alfred 'll be going through Wicklow before he comes here to Ballarat. And all those stupid Irishmen 'll be out waving their flags at the German Queen's son, and getting blind drunk to celebrate. No wonder we're bond, lad. We've no sense.'

Helena had expected an aged and withered man to be in attendance at the herbalist's shop. Instead, she was greeted by a smart looking Chinese of about her own age, plump, obviously prosperous, and with nothing of the fawning Oriental about him. He must have been surprised that this expensively dressed young woman should have chosen to honour his shop, but quickly, in very passable English, he asked whether he could help her.

'I – I have a friend,' she began, and stopped, embarrassed. I expect, she thought, conscious of her flushing face, that he thinks I am going to ask advice about ending a pregnancy. 'She is childless.'

There was just a flicker across that plump, round face. She had thought aright.

'Chinese remedies can cure most things. Not all things.'

'My friend has – once. She lost the child

following a fall. Her health is good other-wise.' Helena became aware of the scratch-ing desperation in her voice, and paused, taking a deep breath. 'She has heard very good reports of your remedies, but she's very shy.'

'In my country, women in that position frequently take the child of another into their home.' The round face was quite impassive. 'In time, the child becomes as their own.'

The tiny, stuffy shop, hung about with dried objects and with rows of pottery jars upon its shelves, was silent now except for the buzz of a fly which had followed Helena in from the dusty, unmade street. After some moments, she found her voice again.

'You mean you have nothing.'

'I could give you a powder. But I would be cheating your friend. I don't practise magic.'

'Thank you for being honest.'

She walked back to Haig's Hotel, conscious of the heat of the November sun which had come through the early morning cloud, and feeling that she had been extremely stupid. She went upstairs to her room immediately, and bathed her face with cool water to help keep back the threatening tears. What a fool she was, building her hopes on a few crushed odds and ends from a Chinese herbalist. She had hurt herself somehow when she had slipped down that companionway on board ship, and she had to accept it. But it was so hard. She loved Harry dearly, and she felt that she had failed him.

To escape her memories, she went out on to the broad veranda which almost circled the hotel at first floor level, and looked out idly into the street, mainly to inspect progress on Ballarat's already famous triumphal archway. Harry would, she knew, ask her about it.

Opposite, a man had stopped his buggy, so that the horse could drink from a public trough at the edge of the roadway. She had a feeling that she knew him, and when a sudden gust of wind caught his hat, revealing red hair for a few moments before he pushed it firmly back into place, she recognised him.

It was the brash Yankee stove salesman who had ogled her at breakfast a few weeks previously. Yet, there was something different about him. What Helena did not know was that Major Doyle had let slip his carefully manufactured part as Sam Doherty. Almost without knowing it, he had regained his

126

austere military bearing, for he was in a hurry to finish his Ballarat business. He knew now that these low, sprawling Australian cities were no good for his purpose, and wanted to head south-west to Wicklow to sound out his chances of finding a confederate. It was in the countryside, with silly yokels waving their little flags, that his chance would come.

He happened to glance up before guiding his horse back into the roadway, and his spine froze within him. This had occurred once before in his life.

It had been early in the war, in Virginia. He had been a mere sergeant then, for his was a battle-won commission. There was a dusty white road twisting through groves of shady trees. They were all tired, following a skirmish which had lasted most of the night, and hot and thirsty into the bargain, for it was July and the height of summer. There had been a farm, unexpectedly, a poor looking place, but there had been a young woman outside, a surprisingly pretty girl, he recalled, for such a ramshackle establishment. She had waved, and they had accepted her offer of fresh well water. But he had had this feeling. She was the evil fairy out of the old stories he had heard as a child, luring men with her looks and enticing words. Sharply, he had ordered his small party to keep moving, but before he could rally those exhausted men, a volley of shots had caught them. As the survivors took cover and fired back, he saw that the girl had already gone, leaving the farm to her Johnny Reb friends. His instinct had been right, and after that, he sometimes trusted it before reason.

He did not recognise Helena as she gazed down into the street from behind her waist high fence of cast-iron flowers and lattice work. His ogling of her at breakfast in that Melbourne hotel dining-room had been merely a repetition of what he had done often in his part as Sam Doherty. He had forgotten her almost immediately, but now, as he stared up at her, he had the most dreadful premonition. This handsome woman in the light, summery dress was his evil fairy, a banshee from the dark shadows, the forerunner of his own doom.

He whipped up the startled horse and went along Sturt Street at a quick canter, sending two children and three dogs bolting for their lives.

Why, he's showing off, thought Helena, amazed, and went indoors to prepare for her delayed midday meal.

Later, Stephen Doyle rationalised his spurt of fear, and put it down to too much cheap whisky too early in the day.

Nine

Naturally, Helena did not mention her futile call at the Chinese herbalist's shop when she returned to Garranbete. However, when she and Harry had dined, and were able to relax pleasantly in the drawing-room for a little while before retiring – and bedtime was seldom late, for early rising had to be the rule at the homestead – she mentioned that she had seen the redheaded Yankee stove salesman in Ballarat.

'Who?' asked Harry, surprised.

'You must remember. A thoroughly obnoxious American who was staying at our hotel in Melbourne.'

'Ah, yes. Well, he must have made an impression on you, Lena. I'd forgotten the fellow. What did he have to say for himself?'

'Oh, I only saw him from a distance. From the upstairs veranda at Haig's.' As soon as she had spoken, she wished she had not mentioned the American. She could hardly tell her husband why Sam Doherty had stuck so vividly in her memory, nor how his glances had made her feel stripped, and exposed … and terribly guilty.

'And quite enough, too,' she added, quickly. 'I hope he's not travelling right through Victoria. I'd hate to find him standing on our doorstep.'

'We've enough peculiar people on our doorstep now,' muttered her husband, and then grimaced, to express his distaste. 'Eggert.'

'What's happened now.' She expected one of the usual sagas about a broken fence, or a confrontation over access to the beach. If she herself ever wished to ride to the beach, she always took care to skirt Eggert's land, but Harry, unfortunately, insisted upon his right of way.

'I'd like to put the brute in gaol where he belongs. I had the pleasure of warning him yesterday. I am a J.P., after all. I was in Wicklow having a chat about the arrangements for Prince Alfred's visit when Eggert drove up in that old cart of his. Had his wife with him. Poor little wretch. There's a baby now. Did you know that?'

Helena nodded. She had known, and,

keeping the fact to herself, had sent a generous gift of clothing to Mrs Eggert.

'Anyone could see Mrs Eggert had been beaten lately. Then all the trouble started. O'Brien came out of the Rose of Tralee, and marched over and asked whether Wes Eggert had been hitting her, and she didn't say a word, just sort of shrunk back into herself like she does, poor thing. Then Eggert told O'Brien to mind his own colonial business, and O'Brien took a swing at him. Then Constable Evans came over and told them to stop it, and O'Brien remembered that his licence is coming up for review soon and went back inside.'

'Poor Mrs Eggert. She's so young, too. I doubt whether she's much past twenty. I wonder why Mr O'Brien interfered.'

'I'm coming to that. I walked over and had a few well chosen words with Eggert. I told him if he started laying violent hands on his wife, he could find himself in a lot of trouble, and he said that she'd fallen over in the dark when she went to attend to the baby. Well, that's his story, and Mrs Eggert's too scared to contradict him. But she certainly fell on a peculiar part of herself.'

'The poor creature.' Helena's exclamation came out involuntarily as she thought of the slightly build Mrs Eggert enduring life in an isolated place with a man her husband was confident was deranged.

'That's the marriage lottery for you. Y'know, Lena, what puzzles me is how Eggert makes a living. For a while, I thought he could be helping himself to my stock, or someone else's, but I've never had a shred of evidence. But he seems to manage on that wretched farm of his, and have enough money over to get himself blind drunk every so often. Still, enough of that. The real reason I went into Wicklow was to have a word with Father Madigan. Lena, come over here.'

He indicated the sofa at his side, and smiling, and willingly, she left her own chair to obey.

'That's better.' He placed his arm about her shoulders, and drew her against him, pressing his mouth into her neck between her collar and the heavy bun of hair suspended in its silken snood.

'You're a lovely woman,' he whispered. 'It hurts to be apart from you for two nights.'

She was not displeased, but curious as to why he had wished to talk with Father Madigan. Harry was no bigot, but neither was he drawn to the Roman faith.

'I had a letter from someone up in Melbourne.' Harry paused, as if debating within himself as to whether he should confide in his wife. 'Someone very close to the top, I might add. Now, you mustn't breathe a word of this to anyone, Lena, but they've picked up rumours, and that's probably all they are, that the Fenians might try some of their tricks while Prince Alfred's in the country.'

'Fenians? Here? Surely not.' Helena, like anyone else who even so much as glanced at a newspaper, had some knowledge of the notorious Irish Republican Brotherhood which was determined to resort to acts of calculated violence and terror in order to gain its goal.

'Wicklow's a chip off the old Irish block. I don't think there are more than half a dozen people in or near the township who aren't as Irish as Paddy's pig. Our poor Constable Evans is definitely odd man out. Nobody would tell him anything. He told me yesterday that he wants nothing more than to be transferred, and I've taken it upon myself to write to the Chief Commissioner of Police suggesting that a constable with an Irish name would be better. Well, after my set-to with Eggert, I had this talk with

Father Madigan. Naturally, he's very much for the wearing of the green, but he's for keeping the law too. He doesn't think any of his flock 'll do anything to disgrace Wicklow's good name. His main worry is trying to keep them all sober on the big day. The Band of Hope brass band is going to play the National Anthem when Prince Alfred arrives, but now it turns out that neither the trombone player nor the drummer have signed the pledge. Father Madigan has tried to get them on to the water wagon, but nothing he says makes the slightest difference, and neither can he find anyone to replace them.'

Thus, Harry had found himself trying to help Father Madigan in his predicament. After all, he wanted the Prince's day in the district to be as pleasant and uncomplicated as possible, and the sensible thing appeared to be to strike at the root of any trouble. Therefore, after a satisfactory chat with the licensee of the Donegal Arms, and with his encounter with Eggert still fresh in his mind, he called on Conan O'Brien at the Rose of Tralee.

This was the quiet part of the day, when the inhabitants of Wicklow were off about their business, ploughing, working on roads, tending stock, gathering up those apparently limitless lumps of volcanic rock from their fields and piling them into fences, or taking their drayloads of sacked potatoes to the small but active port of Warnambool some miles to the east.

Harry found O'Brien at work on his accounts in his own sitting-room behind the public part of the building. The room, except for the mess of papers on the flat table top which served as desk, was pin neat. The publican was a bachelor, but his domestic wants were met by a competent housekeeper. Harry contrasted the scene mentally with that which had been typical of the house before O'Brien had taken over fifteen months previously. Then, the establishment had been little better than a pigsty, and had been known locally as The Bloodhouse, a haunt of disreputable characters and those old hands who still survived from the bad days of convict labour.

'Why, Mr Radford.' Conan O'Brien stood up, his open, freshly coloured face breaking into a smile which just as immediately vanished to be replaced by a look of some concern. 'I hope you haven't called about what happened an hour ago.'

'No, Mr O'Brien.'

The publican seemed eager to proffer an explanation, and so Harry let him say his piece.

'I knew Mrs Eggert some years ago in Melbourne,' said O'Brien. 'As a matter of fact she and I had what you could call an understanding. Then she married Wes Eggert. I always thought her aunt pushed her into it, but...' He shrugged. 'It's all water under the bridge now, but it still upsets me to think she's not as happy as she could be. Eggert is a queer character, all right. But it's none of my business now, and I'll not lose my head agin. It doesn't help Katie – Mrs Eggert – none, and I don't think she wants it, anyhow.'

Harry gave a brief nod of understanding, though privately he thought that O'Brien was a little over-eager to convince him that any regard he had for Katie Eggert was 'all water under the bridge.' Still, it could well be. She was a brown mouse of a woman, and with that miserable look to her which seemed to act as a spur to wife-beaters like Eggert.

'What I wanted to talk about,' said Harry, 'was Prince Alfred's visit. You know that he'll be coming through Wicklow on his way to my own place. It'll be during the morning if all goes well. I think we should all pull together in this, Mr O'Brien, and show a sober face to His Royal Highness.'

'I keep an orderly house, Mr Radford. You know that.' O'Brien was not pleading a cause. He was stating a fact.

'I know. A credit to you. But – well, I was talking to Father Madigan a while ago. He's a bit concerned about the brass band. Some of the members aren't all temperance men, it turns out.'

O'Brien laughed.

'I know the ones you mean. I'll keep an eye on them beforehand.'

'Thanks.' Radford made to leave, but then, as an apparent, but carefully planned afterthought, he turned back. 'You haven't noticed any hotheads, talking in the bar perhaps, who might do something foolish?'

'Foolish, Mr Radford?'

The publican had risen, plainly with the intention of seeing his visitor to the door, and now his ruddy, handsome face showed plainly his bafflement at the question. He's a good-looking fellow, thought Harry, irrelevantly, a bit of a devil with the girls, I'll hold. Funny about Katie Eggert.

'Well, most of your customers are Irish,

and there's been a lot of talk about what's going on overseas. Those fellows who were executed – the Manchester Martyrs – and all the rest of it. Wicklow's a nice, law-abiding little place, and we're all Victorians here, as far as I'm concerned.'

'Fenians, you mean, Mr Radford? Now, you know what Irishmen are like. A few drinks in them, and they'll argue from here to the North Pole. If you mean someone might get it into their head to blow up your picnic – I reckon most of Wicklow 'll be too drunk that afternoon to care.'

'As long as they're not drunk when Prince Alfred drives through.'

Harry picked up his hat, and followed by O'Brien, strolled out into the street. Later, as he told Helena, he realised that O'Brien had not come out with a straight answer, and he wondered whether he ought to write to his influential friend up in Melbourne suggesting that the Prince have an increased police guard as he passed through the very Irish district about Wicklow. Helena, who thought of Wicklow as practically the end of the world, was inclined to laugh at the notion of anything dramatic happening there, but Harry decided to write his letter in the morning.

Helena lay awake for some time. She was overtired, for the journey from Ballarat, partly by coach, and finished in a dogcart sent to meet herself and Miss McPherson ('All this for just *one* day in Ballarat, Mrs Radford!') had been exhausting for them both. To add to their discomfort, it had been a steamily warm day, and as so often happens when one is very weary, her mind, contrarily, was now active to an extreme.

For some reason, she could not stop thinking about the Yankee stove salesman. When she had seen him for the first time in Melbourne, she had been the one to feel the fear. His eyes, sensual and searching, and yet, as cold and terrifying as the icebergs of the great southern ocean, had seemed to penetrate into the very depths of her conscience, bringing out those secrets she had tried to bury. But, yesterday, when he had looked up as she stood behind the iron lace railing, in some eerie and inexplicable manner, the tables had been turned. *He* had been the one to be frightened.

The more she turned it over, and each time she brought out her little mental picture of the man looking up towards her, she became more positive that this was so. He had not been showing off when he had whipped his horse along Ballarat's main street. He had wanted to be out of her sight as quickly as possible. Why?

Could they have met somewhere else, earlier, perhaps in England? She racked her memory, but could not recollect him at all in a context outside Australia. Was it possible that he had known her by sight, been told about her by a mutual acquaintance, a servant perhaps? Did he *know*?

Lying there in a room just dimly illuminated by the half moon beyond the windows shielded by heavy curtains, with the strong, solid body of her husband by her side, Helena Radford tried to suppress the dry sob in her throat.

Somewhere, outside, an owl screeched, setting up a chain reaction of little night noises, and, as had happened so frequently before, the hot tears scalded silently down her cheeks.

Ten

Prince Alfred had arrived in Victorian waters, and the Radfords, Mr and Mrs Rowland, and Mr and Mrs Robert and their children, all packed and headed for Melbourne.

In the capital, excitement rushed through the streets like waves before a storm. One of the results of the great gold rush was a large new middle-class, monied, not very cultured, but ravenous for social advancement, while at the same time labouring under an outsize inferiority complex. Everything in Melbourne just had to be better than anywhere else graced by His Royal Highness's presence.

The gas company worked feverishly to finish the illuminations, and that startling innovation, electric lighting, was wired ready for its Melbourne debut at Parliament House. Dressmakers stitched until their eyes reddened, and every man who owned one brushed his silk hat until it shone. On the side, the preparations for the great free banquet went ahead, with the most enormous quantities of food and drink being gathered for the enjoyment of Melbourne's poor, who, it was anticipated, would consume their victuals in quiet refinement, whilst being watched over by Prince Alfred, rather like a large flock of sheep under the benign eye of their master.

Everyone was quite determined to make the visitor welcome, including such minority groups as the German migrants, who saw Prince Alfred, Duke of Edinburgh, as the heir to the tiny principality of Saxe-Coburg-Gotha. They were to be especially gratified later when His Royal Highness addressed their representatives in fluent German. Other groups within the Melbourne community also went out of their way to preserve their own identity while welcoming a son of the Queen they acknowledged as ruler. The Catholic Irish, helped by the gas company, erected a huge green harp over St Patrick's Hall, incorporating the Gaelic greeting, *Caed Mile Failtichs.* Thus, while greeting Prince Alfred with one hundred thousand welcomes, they made it quite clear that they were a people apart.

Just around the corner from St Patrick's Hall, Melbourne's Ulstermen were less subtle. They decorated their headquarters with a large transparency of King William the Third riding victorious at the Battle of the Boyne.

This obstreperous flourish did not go unobserved. The Hibernian Club seethed.

In Ballarat, Major Doyle smiled thinly to himself as he read about this sectarian hostility in a letter from a Melbourne acquaintance. Ah, Irishmen, he thought, you never change. Who wears the orange and who wears the green matters not at all. What matters is Ireland, our mother country. How much longer must she remain smothered by the alien colours of red, white and blue? You fight over King Billy and King James, dead to dust both of them, and forget the present. You come to blows over the past, forgetting that you still must bow to a German Queen with a German brood they call English.

He folded away the letter, and taking up his bag, and that special case, left his room.

'Have a good trip,' his landlady called after him. 'And remember, you're always welcome here, Mr Doherty.'

She was thoroughly sincere. Mr Doherty was quiet, tidy, and paid up his board on the dot. She wished there were more like him.

The Radfords had jointly rented a house

for the occasion. Perhaps it was not an arrangement which brought joy to the two Mesdames Radford, but their husbands both disliked Melbourne's indifferent hotels and preferred both the comfort and privacy of a house with some of their own staff. At one stage, Ailsa had urged her husband to buy or build a town house, but for once he had been firm. They would use it no more than four weeks a year, he pointed out, and he did not like the idea of renting out his house and his furniture to strangers in order to keep the dwelling aired and lived-in. At least, this was the reason officially handed out by Ailsa. Nearer the truth was that the construction of their vast Western District mansion, with every fitting having to be carried a long distance from the capital, had exhausted their immediate financial resources.

As for Harry, he had never felt the need for a permanent town address. Town was all right for short periods, but his heart was in the country.

Still, the house, situated at the fashionable end of Collins Street in the city, was quite satisfactory in view of the acute shortage of accommodation with Prince Alfred's visit so imminent. For her part, Helena made it her business to be out sightseeing or shopping or visiting as much as possible. Ailsa made no secret of her grievance, and her husband did not improve her humour by pointing out that at least they were spared the expense of the royal entertainment.

Ailsa would have willingly gone to the poorhouse to have the satisfaction of being *the* Mrs Radford who had played hostess to a son of Queen Victoria. For her, not the least aggravating part was that no one else in her family seemed to be worried about the snub. The children all liked Uncle Harry and Aunt Lena, and considered the idea of an outdoors picnic meal far jollier than the indoors banquet their mother would have organised, and at which they would not have been permitted to be present. A picnic meant that, provided they did not overstep the bounds of behaviour expected of them, they could be there with everyone else, eating the same food as Prince Alfred, and finding out whether he ate with a golden fork, or had other peculiarities.

Now, Ailsa had not been quite idle whilst recovering from the shock of learning that she had been bypassed. She had friends in Melbourne, far more friends than a recent arrival such as Helena could expect to have.

She had been busy with her pen, writing letters to everyone she knew who had any social influence, and as a result, she was one of the matrons designated to serve the multitude at the free banquet. Admittedly, most of the voluntary waitresses were younger than Ailsa, but her position was more that of a chaperon, as she explained, or, as her brother-in-law remarked to Lena, a sergeant major.

'It'll suit her down to the ground,' commented Harry. 'She loves ordering people about.'

Ailsa, however, could think only of that delicious moment when she would be presented to Prince Alfred. Oh, they would be guests at the State Ball on the previous night, but such functions were stiff and formal. At the free banquet, when he came to compliment the wealthy women who had so generously given of time and effort so that Melbourne's poor could share in the joys of a royal visit, she did not doubt for an instant that words, perhaps even sentences, would be exchanged. Then, at the Garranbete picnic, she would be in a far better position than Helena. She would have already met Prince Alfred, and be able to state the fact.

Preparing for the State Ball, Helena had

doubts about her dress. Perhaps she should have come up to town to have it made. Ballarat, after all, was a provincial city. She had chosen the design from the latest fashion plates, but, staring at her reflection in the cheval mirror after Miss McPherson had hooked her into it, she was assailed by doubts. It was the first time in her life that she had worn a dress which did not have a completely circular hem. The front panel of this blue silk taffeta dress with detail picked out with bands of black lace, followed the lines of her figure. The rest of the skirt was held out by an enormous crinoline, dipping into a train at the back, but the time of change from the lampshade silhouette which had been in style since Queen Victoria's accession was creeping in, shyly. Perhaps it was symbolic. The crinoline was a cage, and the first daring souls of new womankind were pushing at the doors into a wider world for their sex.

Harry, already resplendent and handsome in his full evening dress, tapped on the door and entered while Miss McPherson was making sure that Helena's elaborately piled-up coiffure was in order.

'Would you leave us for a few minutes? We've plenty of time.'

The maid left, with a curt reminder that time and tide wait for no man.

'She thinks that she owns you,' laughed Harry, and then brought forth the hand he had been holding behind his back, showing Helena the jeweller's box grasped therein.

'As this is a very special occasion, Lena,' he murmured, and unclipped the clasp. Her little gasp as she saw the contents made him smile anew. Moments later, she was regarding her reflection, embellished by the glittering stones about her neck.

'Oh, Harry.' Yet, her lips trembled a little. 'You've been very extravagant. They're – oh, they're beautiful.'

'As I said, Lena, it's a special occasion. And something else too. I want to thank you for making me so happy.'

She turned and put her arms about his neck, hiding her face against his shoulder.

'That's all I've wanted to do, Harry,' she said, in a muffled voice. 'I – I've so wanted to make you happy. Sometimes I feel that I'm a failure.'

He gently eased her from him, looking down at her, holding her hands clasped together in his.

'A failure? Oh, Lena, what a thing to say.'

Yet, he understood what she meant. Her

continuing childlessness was something which he knew weighed heavily on her mind. It troubled him often to see the shadows in her eyes, the almost resigned sorrow as she looked at another woman's child.

'Lena,' he continued, 'I like things the way they are. You must believe me.' He laughed, half ruefully. 'I've grown a bit set in my ways, I expect. And I've plenty of nephews to carry on at Garranbete.'

He was being absolutely truthful. He had grown set in his ways. Helena had brought with her a gift of serene domesticity. Everything at Garranbete was well run, and in perfect taste. They were, as well as lovers, loving companions, and because his marriage was so contented and happy, his bitter feelings about Ailsa's plans for the future had faded. He was especially fond of young Albert, Robert's youngest son, now a sturdy child of seven years. In Albert, he found a little of himself, that silly romantic streak which turned a wrecked sealing vessel into a Spanish galleon, and a barren, flat-topped rock several miles out from the shore into an enchanted misty isle.

Harry Radford could take Albert out and tell him the stories he had heard from the blacks in the old days, strange tales about monsters in the swamps and flames coming from the extinct volcano now called Tower Hill over Warnambool way. Albert listened, fascinated, but the other children were as pragmatic as their parents, Robert and Ailsa.

Now, Harry's wife looked at him, and her full, sweet mouth widened into a smile. For just a fleeting instant Harry remembered that there had been a time, brief though it was, when he had seen in his adored wife a resemblance to the enigmatic Mona Lisa, a hint of secrets concealed. How ridiculous that had been. His dearest Lena was reserved with strangers, that was all.

'Oh, Harry, you're the nicest man in all the world,' she declared, and stretching up a little, kissed him on the lips.

For them both, the night was one of enchantment.

The State Ball was held in the Exhibition Buildings, decorated for the occasion with fernery and fountains arranged into a garden setting. The function was, of course, very formal, but the good looking young Prince seemed to enjoy himself.

'So handsome, and so poised,' gushed Ailsa, her bright gaze fixed upon Helena's diamond necklace. One could almost see her mind working. How long had Helena possessed this bauble? How had it happened that she, Ailsa, had never seen it before, or was it a special gift for the occasion? Or had she bought it herself with Harry's hard won money?

It irritated Ailsa enormously, and almost ruined her evening, except that on several occasions she managed to stand within two feet of the guest of honour. She liked to think that she actually caught his eye once.

Inside the ballroom all was glitter and decorum and decently subdued excitement, with colonial matrons doing their best not to stare too obviously, and, if they had single daughters present, sending up prayers which were unlikely to be answered. Some thought that he looked so like poor, dear Albert the Good, his father. Others considered that the Duke of Edinburgh and likely heir to Saxe-Coburg-Gotha more closely resembled the Queen, his mother. Most shuddered at the very notion that he bore the slightest likeness to those dreadful men, the dear Queen's uncles. No one present would have dream of calling him the Duke of Auld Reekie,* as did the vulgar press and the vulgar poor.

*Slang term for Edinburgh.

Whilst this superhuman refinement filled the Exhibition Building and the band played waltzes, quadrilles and polkas with military precision, disturbing events were taking place no more than a few hundred yards away. Stephen Street, a very mixed thoroughfare running north to south through Melbourne, was not only the home of the town's most notorious brothels, but also boasted the Victorian headquarters of the Royal Orange Lodge.

The opposing faction had tried to be tolerant about that great illuminated picture of King William the Third, but, just as it is a human failing to bite on a bad tooth to find out if it is still hurting, or to lift a scab to see how the sore is getting along underneath, the wearers of the green could not resist passing the Royal Orange Lodge building. Tonight, there were more persons abroad than usual. Like everyone else, Irishmen had flocked into the city, not only to see the illuminations and to stroll the gaudily decorated lanes of the Fitzroy Gardens, but to catch a glimpse of Prince Alfred and Victoria's notables arriving at the Exhibition Building for the State Ball.

Since the Prince's advent, the weather had been unusually warm for November, which is a month offering temperatures ranging from positively wintry to the torrid in those latitudes. The warmth made it not only ideal to wander about the city of an evening admiring the decorations, but also provoked thirsts.

There were afterwards many conflicting stories about what actually happened outside the premises of the Royal Orange Lodge that night, but whatever the beginnings, by the time the fracas was dispersed, a man was dead with a bullet through his body, and several had been badly injured. Others were dragged off to cool down in the city watch-house. The newspapers blamed the Fenians. The shot came from somewhere inside the lodge building. It was an ugly scandal, and neither forgotten nor forgiven for a long time.

Eleven

The morning after the ball, which was the day of the free banquet in Melbourne, and a public holiday, Ailsa Radford arrayed herself in the neat white gown, which, with a blue rosette, constituted the uniform of those select ladies who were to attend to the needs of the populace. Her husband would have preferred to have returned immediately to their home, with his brother and sister-in-law, for he was no longer fascinated by triumphal arches, electric lights, firework displays, and the like. As far as he was concerned, this was not his regular holiday season, and there was much that needed attention elsewhere. As well, he was inclined to be cynical about Melbourne's poor, and doubted whether the presence of the clergy, society women and a prince would have the edifying effect expected by press and organisers alike.

He made vocal his thoughts about the free wine and ale. Robert based his predictions upon the behaviour he had long noticed at parties, weddings, and the like.

'I've seen men who swore they were lifelong abstainers getting 'emselves as drunk as bloody owls when the booze is free,' he affirmed, with that bluntness which so often made his wife shudder. In her opinion, they had come up in the world, and Robert should have tried harder to behave like the splendid gentlemen in the novels about English society which she so enjoyed.

Tersely, and with some concern, he went on to warn Ailsa that 'you must bolt as if Old Nick's after you if the crowd gets nasty.'

There were times, she thought, when Robert was really very trying. At least Rowland, whatever his other faults, had acquired a little polish.

The weather was less than perfect for the occasion, and Dr Smith, organiser in chief whose brainwave the venture had been, looked uneasy as the 'waitresses' set out the vast amounts of food on about half a mile of trestle tables arranged in a semi-circle about the tents and marquees which formed the headquarters of the operation. The venue was conveniently close to the railway station and St Kilda Road which was one of the chief means of access into the city from the sprawling suburbs. At the best of times, this reserve was not much better than a cow paddock, sparsely grassed and dotted with gum trees. Today, with a hot northerly stirring up dust, it was far from pleasant as a locale. Still, as the optimists amongst the organisers remarked, it could have been worse. It could have been raining.

Nonetheless, the wine fountains, fed from hoses leading down from barrels propped in the trees, lent a very picturesque touch to the scene. The white uniformed helpers were accorded special privileges as far as beverages went, and instead of the ordinary red wine donated by local vignerons, several cases of champagne had been placed in the tents which served as their retiring rooms. This, of course, was not to be broached until the contented and grateful poor had wended their blissful way homewards.

Early in the day, unease began to seep through committee and helpers alike. The poor, arriving in droves from all directions, were much more numerous than one would have supposed in Marvellous Melbourne. Also, some of them were remarkably strong and well dressed in looks, and scattered through the throng were far too many of those flashy young toughs known as 'larrikins', accompanied by their female followers, 'donahs'.

By midday, the sun was glaring down hotly, and the crowd was pressed against the barriers which were intended to keep them back from the tables until Prince Alfred arrived at half past two.

From the sheltering tents, the ladies watched in some trepidation. Few of them had ever seen so many people together in one place before, and certainly never so many people whose perspiring faces grew increasingly red and cross as they looked across the barriers at those laden tables which were now the target for swarms of hungry bush flies. Dr Smith, bustling about with that 'trust me' air which had made him a fortune in his mail order medicine business, assured them that everything would be all right when the young Prince arrived, as he should very soon.

So, the ladies in white waited, although some of them expressed aloud their doubts as to how they would be able to serve so many people. Ailsa, whose less attractive side was not obvious to those who met her casually, passed the time in cheerful chatter and gossip with those about her. She was a little older than most of the others, which gave her a pleasing feeling of leadership. The interlude of waiting also brought her way some information which she would mull over very carefully later.

The crowd by now was of enormous proportions, and some of the wilder spirits pushed forward towards the wine fountains, but happily, Ailsa and some of the other women were able to persuade them, gently, to return to their side of the barriers. But the elaborate marquee set up to provide Prince Alfred with a secluded eating place remained empty. Another hour crept past, and during that hour an event unknown to the organisers took place. The police chief had ridden from the Governor's residence, Toorak House, where the Prince was staying, and a few shocked moments set his imagination to work. He saw His Royal Highness being trampled to death, or worse still, attacked by one of the Fenians who supposedly had instigated the 'Stephen Street Outrage' the previous night.

Therefore, upon returning to Toorak House, he described the situation briefly, and added his opinion that it would be folly for the Prince to attend, as it would be impossible to provide sufficient police protection. His advice was taken, and a mounted trooper sent off immediately to advise the organisers of the banquet that Prince Alfred would not be attending.

'How is Mrs Rowland Radford?' asked a young woman of Ailsa as they all waited, anxiously trying to see past the hard packed multitude to the road along which Prince Alfred was supposed to be coming.

'Quite well, thank you.' Ailsa did not wish to be reminded of Helena. That diamond necklace rankled. At the same time, she was curious. She did not know the questioner, a slight, fair girl still in her early twenties, with the marked accent of one not so long from England.

'She has a family now?'

'A family? Oh, you mean children. No, Helena is childless.'

'What a pity. We had adjoining staterooms on the voyage out, you know. My maid, Nanny I call her still because she was my nurse when I was small, helped nurse Mrs Radford after her – well, accident. Her own maid was a young girl, quite inexperienced, and I willingly lent her Nanny Hudson.'

Ailsa had heard most of this before from Helena, and was not very interested in hearing it again, until her new acquaintance said something which quite took her attention away from the growing sounds of discontent arising like an unmusical overture from the huge crowd pressing hungrily against the barriers. So. Ailsa turned mental handsprings at the sheer delicious scandal of it. So.

Now the moment of crisis for the free banquet had arrived. Dr Smith, shattered inwardly but outwardly brave, announced that Prince Alfred was unable to attend, and his words were followed by a roar, cracking noises as the barricades gave way, and finally by the rumble of thousands of feet rushing towards the laden trestles. A disinterested observer might have commented that the news that Prince Alfred would not be coming had caused no disappointment amidst the crowd. They were simply hungry, thirsty, and tired of waiting.

A reporter wrote in the staider morning newspaper the following day that 'We saw a bacchanalian picture of unbelievable horror, set against the general background of struggling carnivora.'

Actually, most of those involved in what the same reporter also described as a 'frightful saturnalia such as we shudder to recall' seemed to be having a very merry time. They tore into the victuals, goodnaturedly tossing legs of lamb, sticks of sausage, loaves of bread and so forth back to those unable to reach the tottering trestles. Some, obviously not up on the finer points of etiquette, drank water from the finger bowls, but most grabbed every receptacle offering, including the leather fire buckets about the tents, and filled them with wine. The most enterprising and agile climbed into the trees and helped themselves to the wine at the source, from the barrels. The sober and thirsty became the drunk and replete in an astonishingly short time, and many of those who had climbed into the trees were soon draped over the limbs of the big old eucalypts, unconscious and uncaring.

To the ladies trembling in the tents, it looked like the Sack of Rome, the Fall of the Bastille, and the Indian Mutiny all in one. Ailsa, who had never lacked physical courage, energetically whacked with her sunshade the first young hooligan to force his way into the tent. Tipsy, and surprised by the strength of this small, plump woman, he staggered backwards into the open air, but others in quest of food, and better still, drink, were not so easily discouraged, nor so naive as to try a frontal assault. They cut the guy ropes, and while the ladies in white were struggling to free themselves from the smothering blanket of canvas, made off with valuables and those cases of champagne meant as a reward for the society waitresses.

Ailsa, emerging from under the canvas, struggled to her feet, and saw two youths, attired in the bell-bottomed trousers and short jackets which were the uniform of the larrikin set, making off with her reticule, her bonnet, and the fur trimmed jacket she had worn over her white gown early that morning before the heat became so oppressive. One of them put her bonnet on his head, and began swaggering about in a mock-feminine fashion.

'Give me that, you rotten young lout,' she screamed, reverting to the instincts of a youth spent in a series of rough mining camps where her father had founded his fortunes. So, while the clergymen, whose presence had been meant to keep the tone of the banquet at a high level, tried to protect the other ladies who swooned and shrank in the mad melee, Ailsa grabbed at her jacket. Because the youth who was holding it tugged just as hard, the garment split in two, sending the pair of them reeling backwards in opposite directions. The youth fell straight into a large apple pie which lay on the ground, Ailsa into the arms of a

162

shocked Methodist minister.

She was not daunted, but as she rushed towards the youth, who was picking himself up out of the wreck of the very large pie, a jet of champagne from a newly opened bottle caught her full in the face.

'Oh, you – you–' spluttered Ailsa, and half-blinded, flung herself in the general direction of her enemy. The first squirt of champagne had been accidental. The second was on purpose, and when Ailsa recovered her vision, she found herself being hustled away from the scene of battle by a policeman.

'Remember yourself, madam, remember yourself,' he repeated several times.

The next morning, Ailsa read in the more conservative of Melbourne's two morning newspapers that the fiasco was 'a demonstration of the natural baseness of the masses.'

She could not read much more, for she was nursing a most obvious black eye.

Elsewhere, Dr Smith, father of the scheme, referred to the chief of police as a chicken-hearted meddler. Throughout Melbourne and suburbs, hundreds of the baser masses endured their hangovers, and agreed that it was a day in a million. Prince or no prince, they would never forget it as long as they lived.

'They can say what they like, I never saw so many happy drunks in all my life,' said Robert cheerfully, as they journeyed back towards Ballarat in the train. When he had heard, in the peace of his club, of the shambles developing at the public feast, he had immediately started forth to rescue his wife, only to be met by a staggering horde waving chunks of food, and occasionally, bottles of champagne. After a fruitless and worrying search, he had in the end returned to their Melbourne lodgings, there to find Ailsa, newly arrived, dirty, dishevelled, her white dress torn and stained with wine, and her right eye puffing up alarmingly. Sad to say, she was not in the state of nervous prostration one would have expected of a lady, but rather, in a rage over the indignities she had suffered.

However, during the train journey to Ballarat the next day, despite being heavily veiled in suffocating heat, she was quite bright, and inclined to Robert Radford's relief, to look on the funny side. She began to relate small incidents in the amusing way which, although most women in her circle were aware of her cattiness, made her popular at social gatherings.

Robert, fortunately, was unaware of the real reason for Ailsa's good spirits. She was cheerful because she had now had time to think over her conversation with the young English woman. With this tucked up her sleeve, Ailsa felt very content.

Twelve

Stephen Doyle read about the disastrous free banquet in a two-days old copy of the Melbourne *'Argus'*, which tinged its account both with disapproval and a crowing certainty of having been right all along about the outcome. He found it amusing. The lower orders had come off best in the encounter, and those who considered themselves superior had been left looking like idiots. However, he wasted little time in savouring the details as he sat in his small upstairs bedroom in a modest hotel at Warnambool, a stone's throw from the busy wharf. That was the sideshow. What really took his attention was the continuing discourse on the 'Stephen Street Outrage'. He was able to pick up much of the drama from the editorial which made no bones about its belief that the Fenian movement was at the back of the episode.

He had missed reading the issue containing the whole story as it came fresh from eye witnesses and the always lurid pens of the colonial journalists. Yesterday, he had been travelling across country, and the night before he had spent at a godforsaken hamlet where papers arrived weekly if at all.

He put aside the newspaper and lay back on his neatly made bed, taking the precaution of removing his boots before placing his feet on the clean white Marcella quilt. Doyle was tired to the bone, and intensely aware of one thing.

He disliked Australia to the point of hatred. He was desperately homesick for America, where nothing was quite so strange to European eyes as here in the southern continent. There was so little gentleness here, and although he had been assured that the countryside had been green only a month since, it was now brown under an increasingly hot sun, with choking clouds of dust thrown up constantly on the unmade roads.

Major Doyle had long considered himself past sentimental feeling, and yet tonight, in this lonely room – and how many lonely rooms there had been – it was only with the greatest effort that he could return his mind to the unceasing dedication which had directed it for so many years. The pictures kept drifting back into his mind, the white clapboard houses, the red barns, the glorious autumn woods of New England, the green meadows and stately mansions of Virginia, and the odd moments of beauty amid the terror and hideousness of battle. He could remember a day spent in a tree. There had been a squirrel in the tree, timid at first, and yet gaining confidence as the hours passed, until it deigned to take a piece of crust from the interloper. At the end of the long wait, after whiling away the time befriending a squirrel, he had shot dead a man riding across the meadow below, the man's horse treading down the spring wildflowers as the beast bore him forward to the exact spot where the bullet would meet his brain, cleanly, killing him instantly.

Stephen Doyle sometimes wondered about that. The man had not been wearing Confederate grey, but Union blue. His own orders had been to wait until a man wearing a Union uniform of colonel's rank, and riding a bay horse, had ridden across the clearing. But at the time, he had not wondered. He had simply obeyed orders, and when he had looked around after firing the shot and seeing his prey die, the squirrel had vanished.

Because his mind was relaxed, the unbidden thought, usually suppressed, came to the surface. I should have gone West with the army after the war. I could have learnt something about the ways of the Indians, and helped them obtain justice.

Why did this idea haunt him so? Had he gone against the dictates of his own destiny in choosing another path?

I'm becoming battle weary, he thought, making the effort to bring his mind back into the present. And I don't particularly like the Irishmen I've met here in Victoria. Perhaps Australian life has softened them, but the Irish here are more concerned with making sure that Catholic schools will receive a government grant than teaching their pupils that Ireland must be free. Perhaps it is because Irishmen have become ministers in the government, or just that the country is never green enough, nor green long enough, to keep Ireland fresh in their minds.

He laughed bitterly to himself about the lofty editorial remarks in the *'Argus'* about Fenian plots. He'd guarantee that he was the only genuine Fenian in Victoria. If there were other true members of the Republican Brotherhood here, they would not be wasting their time throwing stones at King Billy's picture outside the Royal Orange Lodge. They'd have burned down Toorak House, with his Excellency the Governor and Prince Alfred inside of it, or blown up the *Galatea* where she lay at anchor.

No, everything depended on him, and the worst of it was that those hotheaded fools with their riot over the picture of a king who had been dead most of two centuries had increased police watchfulness over the royal visitor.

It was almost dinner time in the small hostelry set back in a street from the harbour, one of the busiest on the Australian coastline, with its outflow of wool, sheepskins, hides and potatoes, and inflow of luxuries for the rich squatters and necessities for ordinary folk.

Stephen Doyle arose with a weary sigh, and combed his hair carefully in front of the mirror. Once again, he had to slip into the personality of Sam Doherty, the brash American, who was everyone's friend, and who, with a cheeky, glue-like persistence, convinced storekeepers that his patent stoves would win every housewife's heart.

Behind the mask of his brashness, he had to watch and listen incessantly. As his acquaintance in Ballarat had told him, there were Irishmen in plenty here on the southwest coast, but too many of them were what Doyle contemptuously called Bog Irish, with no mind for anything beyond food and drink, especially drink. Continuously, he was carefully studying Prince Alfred's progress in the newspapers. For the nonce, His Royal Highness had finished his round of duties in Melbourne, and was now commencing his Western District tour. After visiting Geelong, the other large port on Port Phillip Bay, the Prince was to be entertained by the wealthy Austins (and their rabbits), before commencing a long and roundabout trip to Ballarat, through Warnambool and Wicklow, and thence across the plains to the gold rush city.

It was time for the Yankee stove salesman to move on to Wicklow. That was the most westerly point of the Prince's travels, and from thence, it was a dogleg back to

170

Ballarat. Doyle knew that he could not arrive in Wicklow too early, for what could Sam Doyle be finding to do in such a tiny dot of a place for more than a day? But he must not cut it too fine, either, for he had to have the time to sound out the man whose name Bill Joyce had given him. If needs be, he could manage without help, but he had to consider that he knew very little of the country. In the confusion following Prince Alfred's assassination, he knew that he had a good chance of escape if he kept his head, but his ignorance of the land itself would be working against him.

The Rose of Tralee, he discovered when he arrived in Wicklow on a hot morning when even the breeze blowing off the ocean across the sand dunes had fallen, was a snug little building. Of weatherboard, it had been painted that depressing shade of pale brown which these Australians favoured rather than the neat white of eastern America. Major Doyle could not make up his mind whether this was because brown paint was cheaper, or because it would not show up the dust which blew so plentifully once spring was past. Still, everything about the Rose of Tralee was tidy. The paling fence at the back, enclosing a private yard, was new and

171

without those broken gaps which seemed to be an obligatory part of Australian fences. The windows were clean, and bunches of white pyrethrum daisies hung from the rafters of the veranda to discourage that all-pervading nuisance, the fly.

'American, aren't you?' The landlord studied the signature in his register after Major Doyle had written 'Samuel Doherty' with considerable flourish. A flashy sales-man had to have a signature to match.

'Nowadays, yes. But I'm a native of that very place this fair little town was named for.'

Conan O'Brien was studying him care-fully, as if trying to size him up. Then:

'I've been told you've a message for me about my brother Desmond,' he said.

Stephen Doyle hid his surprise. He had not quite expected this straightforward approach, and he assessed the handsome publican carefully. He seemed an open, frank sort of fellow, and Doyle decided to sound out where O'Brien's loyalties lay very carefully before confiding in him. He distrusted adult persons with that honest, almost naive look to them. It was usually a carefully cultivated pose.

'You heard from Mr Joyce?' he asked.

'Yes. When you've settled in, will you join me in my private parlour?'

Private parlour had an elegant sound to it, but the room was the same in which Harry Radford had interviewed O'Brien, a clean, comfortable and plain chamber no more than nine feet square. Doyle glanced about covertly, looking for religious pictures. There were none, which was a relief. The Church and Fenianism were not compatible.

The landlord pushed a bottle of Irish whiskey across the table towards his guest. Doyle much preferred the American bourbon variety, and he hoped the quality was better than that of the liquor he had drunk with Bill Joyce in Ballarat.

'To Ireland and her sons,' said O'Brien, lifting his glass.

'To Ireland's martyrs,' responded the other man, and took a wary sip. It was good whiskey.

O'Brien did not waste time.

'If Bill Joyce sent you to me, it was for a reason, and not about my brother, either.'

'What makes you say that?'

'My brother's name was Dermot. The one who blew himself up at Clerkenwell, that is.'

Doyle could have kicked himself. Now that he thought back to his conversation with the bedridden Joyce, he recollected quite well that the name of O'Brien's brother had never been mentioned. Why had he picked on the name Desmond? Something else he and Joyce had discussed as they emptied the bottle, most likely. There was one thing he could not doubt. Conan O'Brien was smarter than he looked.

'And Dermot was the truest lieutenant the Republican Brotherhood ever had. What's your game, Yankee?'

Doyle looked down at his glass, still almost untouched, for he was not going to fall into that trap again. He turned it about in his hands, still not sure how far he should venture with this fresh-faced young man.

'I'm a stove salesman,' he stated. 'What we call a drummer in the States. A commercial traveller in British countries.'

'You won't find much business in Wicklow. You'd do as well to stay in Warnambool. That's where most people round here go if they want more than a few odds and ends. Or up to Ballarat.'

Doyle knew that they could go on skirting about his real business indefinitely, but he was not ready yet to commit himself.

'I've been in Warnambool. A busy port. If a man wanted to leave the country in a hurry, I daresay he could find a ship to take him on to, say, Sydney.'

'And you're thinking of leaving in a hurry?' O'Brien took a very small sip of his whiskey. 'After killing Prince Alfred, perhaps?'

Doyle controlled the intense shock he felt. The other was far shrewder than he had suspected at first. But, could he be trusted? Because he had had a brother killed for the cause was no criterion. Look at the Lalor family, members on either side.

'That's a strange thing to be saying.'

'Not so strange. You're Irish, American, and a Fenian, if I'm not mistaken. What else could have brought you here to Wicklow? Nothing's happened in Wicklow since they planted the first potato. The only excitement here is the temperance society's band practice every week. The only thing worth happening in Wicklow hasn't happened yet – and that's Prince Alfred passing through on his way to Garranbete to have a meal with the Radfords. The Radfords own pretty well everything hereabouts, by the way.'

'Would these Radfords be interested in a stove?'

'Hard to say. Harry's house was brand new four years ago, and from what I've heard – I wasn't here then – he didn't spare any expense in getting everything that was up to date, bathrooms and all. The road to Garranbete goes west out of Wicklow, a bit back from the coast, for perhaps three miles, and then turns north. The river comes down and turns there, you see, before flowing this way behind the hummocks for quite a way. The Radford place – Mr Harry's, that is, Mr Robert's further inland – is about three and a half miles upstream. The road turns right by Eggert's farm. Loneliest place you'd ever find, and a lot of uncleared bush still behind the sand dunes.'

Now, is this his way of trapping me, thought Doyle. Putting the idea into my head? But he knew that he would be out on the morrow to inspect the land about Eggert's farm.

'I can give you a name in Warnambool,' continued O'Brien.

Doyle felt the rush of triumph through his being. After weeks of frustration, the way was being shown him. Yet, he forced himself into caution. He considered that the true reason for most Irish failures was the lack of careful planning. Irish rebels seized upon a grand idea, and then rushed at it without another thought. An ounce of foresight was worth a hundredweight of courage.

Thirteen

Helena could not have, in her direst imaginings, have guessed the upheaval the Prince's proposed visit would cause in her quiet, well-ordered home. She had been seized by that obsession, common to persons whose houses are to be honoured by the presence of the mighty, that the distinguished visitor would personally inspect every nook and cranny. Therefore, the whole of the big house had to be scrubbed and polished, from top to bottom. It was most unlikely that His Royal Highness would inspect the attics, for instance, but even those normally unused were ruthlessly spring cleaned, and many a spider which had considered that it had found a cosy retreat was either slaughtered or exiled.

Aided by her usual servants and some extra women from Wicklow, Helena saw to it that the whole house smelt of and gleamed with cleanliness.

'I don't think he'll be looking about

inside,' said Harry, somewhat aghast at the discomfort caused by this upheaval.

'It could rain on the day,' said Helena gloomily. The trouble with all this cleaning was that nothing seemed to have gone back into its right place, and there was a difficulty in finding articles which custom decreed were always to be located in a particular spot.

'Liked it better as it was before,' grumbled Harry, sitting down in his favourite chair, and absentmindedly hooking out a boot to drag the piano stool forward, it being his intention to rest his boots thereon.

'Harry.' It was not so much a reprimand as a distressed wail. Helena loved her husband dearly, but this did not blind her to certain domestic weaknesses which had been implanted long ago, when furniture in the Radfords' pioneer shack had consisted mostly of rough makeshifts and old chests.

'I'm going to be glad when it's all over,' muttered Harry. He meant it from the bottom of his heart. The matter of fencing off a suitable piece of river bank had seemed simple at the time, but with the dry spell, the water level had fallen, and at some time during the previous night, several cattle had found their way there across to the protected meadow. Not only had they munched heartily at the grass so carefully preserved, but they had left behind indisputable evidence of their visit. The very notion of an accident to a royal boot was enough to turn Harry cold. He was a tough man of the land, long accustomed to taking everything associated with animal husbandry in his stride, but he shared with the rest of humanity the common mania of needing to have everything absolutely perfect for royalty.

So, precious hours had been wasted that day in removing anything distasteful from the picnic site, and two men, who should have been more sensibly employed, were put to work carting water in buckets from the river, and watering the damaged grass in the faint hope that it would turn into smooth sward within three days. An addition to the fence had been hastily constructed along the edge of the river, and now Harry was working out timetables in his head. When should those fences be whipped away, giving the impression that the picnic site was a natural and untouched glade, early enough for the Prince not to see the artifice, and yet late enough to prevent another disaster like the one of the previous night?

The ordinary stock could be kept well away during the day of the picnic, but about the homestead there was a largish population of domestic cows, geese, hens, dogs, cats, and so forth. They would all have to be rounded up and incarcerated for the duration of the Prince's visit. There was one hen in particular, Old Biddy, who, having passed her egglaying days, and somehow escaped the stock pot, now imagined in her dotage that she was a rooster. In addition, she was fond of human company, and had been known to invite herself to a family teaparty out under the trees, leaping on to the back of a chair, and emitting a travesty of a crow.

Old Biddy could be counted upon to convulse Harry's nephews and nieces, and any other visiting children. How would she affect a member of the House of Guelph?

'Ailsa is coming over tomorrow to help me with the final preparations,' said Helena, moving nervously about the room, and readjusting the bric-à-brac for the dozenth time.

'Oh, no,' groaned Harry, wrenching himself away from the nightmare vision of Old Biddy flapping about on a table, right in front of Prince Alfred.

'Well, she offered, and she *is* bringing over

extra silver, and so forth.'

'Watch out, Lena. She'll cut you out altogether if she has half the chance.'

Helena was aware of that, and secretly dreaded Ailsa's company on the next day. It was all too obvious that she had not really forgiven Harry and his wife for snatching away this social plum, although the snatching had been quite involuntary. If Helena had known exactly what Ailsa had in store, she would have been still more apprehensive. For now, her main anxiety was that, on the great day, Ailsa would man-oeuvre herself into the position of appearing to be the hostess. And Ailsa, thick skinned and determined on social aggrandisement, was quite capable of doing just that.

Yet, nobody could have been sweeter than Ailsa when she arrived with her boxes of china (and nothing second rate, either; she had brought her very best), silver and linen. Her whole manner seemed to say that she had accepted the way things had turned out, and now, as a member of the Radford family, she would do her best to make the occasion a resounding success.

For her part, Helena was glad of Ailsa's help, for Robert's wife was undoubtedly competent, and a born organiser. She planned strategy with a skill which, transferred to an army officer, would have ensured a field-marshal's baton in record time. Nothing could go wrong, it appeared now, except the weather, and even if that proved disappointing, the indoor plan could be put into operation without too much difficulty.

The two women sat down to afternoon tea in what was apparently closer amity than ever before.

'I thought Rowland usually came in to tea,' remarked Ailsa, as Helena poured.

'Only if he's working near the homestead.' Helena smiled. 'It does seem strange to me. The great landowners back Home leave the work to their agents, but I'm afraid the habit of supervising absolutely everything is ingrained in Harry.'

Ailsa bit into a featherweight scone, oozing melted butter. Something which she regretted was that now that she had risen in the world, she no longer did her own cooking, and no person she hired was quite as good as herself in the kitchen. Helena was luckier than herself when it came to hiring cooks.

'Well, I don't suppose that Rowland had much time to warn you about life in Victoria before you were married,' she said. 'How long did you know him? Only about three months, wasn't it?'

'Three months. Oh, no, only three weeks.' Helena laughed. 'Looking back, I'm amazed that I took such a risk. But I think that I knew that he was a fine man the first time I saw him.'

There was a shadow on the carpet near the open French windows, but neither of the women noticed, for suddenly, there was a tenseness between them as Helena saw the hardness in Ailsa's hazel eyes.

'How strange,' said Ailsa quietly. 'I had thought it was three weeks. That's what Rowland told us, and Blanche too, when she wrote. But I met someone you know on that absolutely ghastly day of the free banquet. Her maid took care of you for a few days after your – er – accident on board ship.'

'Oh yes,' responded Helena, far too quickly. 'It was most kind of her. Mrs Matthews, wasn't it? She sent her own maid in to help nurse me. The girl I had as personal maid then had absolutely no experience in that sort of thing.'

Ailsa helped herself to sugar from the gleaming silver bowl, and stirred it into her tea, moving her spoon far longer than necessary as she looked down, and then, smiling slightly, across at Helena.

'And I believe it's quite dreadful to lose a child in the fourth month. Fortunately, I've been spared such an ordeal, but I believe one can be quite ill.'

Helena knew that she had gone deathly white. All the guilt, the fears with which she had grappled and tried to push aside, had now risen to grip her so that she could not think clearly. She wanted desperately to say something light, to sweep it all away, to pretend that it was nothing at all, but she could not find a word to utter.

Ailsa kept smiling, and leaned across the table, to place a consoling hand on Helena's forearm.

'Oh, it's all in the past,' she murmured. 'I'm sorry I mentioned it.' A lie, of course. She was enjoying Helena's discomfiture enormously. 'Don't let it fret you. We all know that Rowland was one for the girls when he was younger – well, Colleen proves that, doesn't she? He married you, and that's all that matters.'

She said this last with such an air of pious earnestness that an onlooker who did not know her could have been forgiven for thinking that Ailsa was being very understanding

184

about Helena's need to marry in a hurry. She looked about, startled, as Harry walked in, flinging his widebrimmed hat on to a chair and pulling out another.

'I'm sorry I'm late, Lena,' he said, and Helena poured another cup of tea, her hands trembling as they lifted the heavy teapot.

When he had left them again, Ailsa announced that she must herself be on her way.

'And I'm so sorry I put my foot in it,' she trilled. 'Believe me, I won't tell a living soul. I don't blame you and Rowland one little bit for your little fib. After all, a seven months baby isn't at all unusual. Young Albert was eight weeks early. It was a worry, but he thrived.'

As she watched Ailsa being driven homewards, Helena put a hand against one of the poles supporting the veranda roof. She felt quite ill, and yet at the same time, she had a hard job suppressing hysterical laughter. She thinks Harry and I had to marry in a hurry, she thought. Going indoors, Helena felt as if every ounce of life had been drained from her being.

This then was the culmination of years of guilt, and the dread that her secret would one day be revealed. The doctor on board ship who had attended her after her fall had been understanding: it was not the first time a woman had implored him to lie a little to save her reputation, and she had not been aware that the servant lent by the occupant of the adjoining stateroom had noticed so much.

For so long, she had considered that there had been something almost miraculous in the way things had worked out. From being in the greatest despair, with no prospects but disgrace and poverty, she had been suddenly rescued and removed to a life of wealth and security.

How, from this distance, could she explain her folly? All considered, was it so hard to understand? Her life had not been a particularly happy one through her teens and most of her twenties. Her mother had died young, and when she was sixteen, her father had taken to wife a girl not much older than Helena herself. She and Eudora were never close, and discomfort in the relationship had not been helped by the family's near poverty.

At eighteen, Helena had been in love with, and unofficially engaged to, the handsome son of a neighbouring small farmer. Her father had objected to the match on the grounds of the young man being socially inferior, and had sent his daughter a hundred miles away to act as companion to an elderly relative. At the same time, he made it clear to the young man that Helena was not for him. Eventually, the young man emigrated to Canada, with another bride. Helena had been bitterly hurt. She had been prepared to defy her father, to elope if necessary, but her suitor's affection had not been strong enough to run against the tide of local opinion.

The old lady to whom she had acted as companion had died, and Helena had taken on a post as governess. The years she had spent with that particular family had been pleasant ones, but the children grew older, and her services were no longer required. It was during her last months there that she met again a distant cousin, whom she had known most of her life, and who was an officer in the Indian Army – and a widower. Some months later, he had proposed by letter, and she had accepted. She was not rapturously in love, but she liked and respected him, and anticipated a happy and rewarding marriage.

By this time she had a new post, in

London, which was less congenial than the last. Arrangements for her passage to India had been made when the letter arrived, telling her that Christopher was dead. She was twenty-seven, a handsome young woman with no money, few prospects, and very aware that her youth was slipping away. Hers was a warm and passionate nature, and now it seemed that a cruel fate had thwarted all her natural yearnings, leaving her nothing ahead but lonely years spent in one dreary post after another.

Andrew had been the young brother of that splendid lady, Helena's employer, who was one of the most elegant women moving through London's most exclusive social circles. She was, it was whispered, the *chère amie* of a well-known political figure, while her husband had also found romantic love elsewhere. It was the way of their world, accepted as long as it was conducted with proper discretion.

Handsome, dashing and married, Andrew was almost penniless, separated from his wife, and for some reason never fully explained, on an extended stay at his sister's home. With accomplished ease, he had set out to amuse himself with the governess. Helena had simply lost her head, urged on by the feeling that this was her last chance to taste love. At the time, it had been a romantic idyll, with secret trysts, meaning glances as they passed one another on the stairs, and at first, sweetly stolen kisses. The first time he came to her room, she was aware that she had only to tell him to go and nothing more would have eventuated, because Andrew was a gentleman as well as a womanizer. Looking back over a number of years, the romance was stripped away, and she saw herself only as the partner in a sordid little intrigue.

Her ladyship had found out, and dismissal had been instant. Within twenty-four hours she was packed and out of that great London mansion, fearfully aware that she was pregnant. Andrew's ardour had cooled almost immediately. Now, it turned out, he was in serious financial trouble, and dependent upon handouts from his sister, who had married so well. Still, he found Helena's lodgings, and sent the wretched young woman to an address where, he assured her, she would be 'fixed up'.

Helena had waited outside the house for an hour, trying to pluck up the courage to go inside. Her orthodox religious upbringing made her believe that she would be compounding her sin by trying to free herself of the consequences, and at the same time, she was frightened by the stories she had heard of girls dying in agony from blood poisoning after abortions. Andrew was furious with her when she gave back the money intended for the abortionist. He told her that he could not afford to help her any more, and in any case, a clergyman's daughter should have had more sense than to place herself in such a predicament.

There was nothing for it but to go home, terrified of the future, too ashamed to tell her family, and living miserably from one day to the next, dreading that inevitable thickening of her figure. She genuinely believed that suicide was the ultimate sin, but on the day when Harry Radford had discovered her standing by the pond, she had been trying to force herself into leaping to her death in the dark, weed-infested waters. She was bargaining with herself. If she went nearer, to that slippery patch of clay, and her foot slid from beneath her, would that be a deliberate taking of her own life?

It was while she was contemplating this, and even edging cautiously towards the water, that she had heard Harry Radford's firm footsteps. When she had been introduced to him after church, she had been too concerned with her own worries to take much notice of him. Now she had the strongest and strangest flash of intuition. This, she thought, is the man I am going to marry. This is the man for whom I have been intended all along. He has come here because he wishes to marry me. He has come to save me.

The day before the wedding, she received a letter from Andrew. He was sorry, he wrote, that he had been so angry with her. Since then, he had had a large win at Newmarket, and his most pressing financial problems had been solved. He suggested that she go abroad, posing as a widow, and after the birth, he would arrange to have the child adopted.

Helena had torn the letter into a dozen pieces, and burnt the scraps in the kitchen stove. Then, not wishing Andrew to write again, or even worse, come in search of her, she had penned a few lines telling her former lover that she was about to marry and travel to another country. No one reading this missive could have interpreted it as other than simple information.

Her miscarriage, so providential, had been

quite accidental. The fact that she had not conceived again she accepted as her continuing punishment, but even that had been eased by her husband's rational attitude.

Had Harry heard the conversation between herself and Ailsa? How long had he been standing outside the French windows? Had their voices been loud enough to carry?

Helena's next few hours were an agony of waiting.

Fourteen

Katie Eggert and Helena Radford were unaware that they had something in common. They had been married upon the same day, and both somewhat suddenly. After this, there was little resemblance in the courses taken by their respective lives, although they lived in circumstances which made them neighbours.

Helena's life seemed set for many years of comfort and social position. For poor Katie, ill-educated, and it had to be admitted, not very bright, life stretched ahead as a grey expanse of poverty and misery. Eggert could have, by better management and less drinking, done reasonably well with his three hundred acre block if he had exerted himself to drain the swampy portions and sow good pasture.

Yet, mysteriously, there was always some money. Every so often, when the storekeeper in Wicklow, and the publican at the Donegal Arms were both threatening to bring in the bailiffs if outstanding accounts were not settled, Wesley Eggert would travel to Melbourne, and as if by magic, he would be solvent again. Once, Katie asked him what he did in Melbourne, but he told her to shut up. It was business, and she would not understand, and anyway, he did not see why he should have to tell a stupid slut like herself everything he did. A more sophisticated person than his wife would have suspected blackmail, but Katie was too scared of him to pry further.

She did her best to be a good wife. She was not lazy, and had an instinct for housekeeping, and the poor shack was always spotless. It might as well have been kept like a pigsty for all the thanks Wesley gave her. He detested her, and never stopped comparing her unfavourably with the beloved first wife who was enshrined in his memory, gaining virtues, as the years slipped past, which she had never possessed. Molly had been bright and lively. Katie was dull and slow. Molly had been pretty. Katie was drab, although the truth was that Katie had good features, and would have been greatly improved if he had spent a little money in keeping her better fed and dressed.

He even hated the poor girl for being a good housewife and remarkably industrious. It gave him less to criticise. When, after quite some time, she timidly announced that she was pregnant, he gave her a good beating for being such a nuisance.

Katie did not expect much from life. She had been superfluous in her aunt's house, and had a generally poor opinion of herself. But, for the little girl born to her on a scorching February morning when the north wind seared down from the great inland plains and the heat haze shimmered on the track, life was going to be different. She did not quite know how it was going to be different, but her darling Maria would never suffer as she had suffered.

Anyway, something had happened to make her happier, although frightened at the same time. Conan O'Brien had taken over one of the two public houses in Wicklow, a few months before Maria was born.

Wesley was furious about it. He accused Katie of deliberately persuading O'Brien to come to the southwest, but he was quite off the mark, for Katie had known nothing of it until she had seen Con standing outside his door during a visit to Wicklow. At first, Katie had no intention of reviving the friendship, and, as far as that went, neither did O'Brien, for a while. His arrival in Wicklow was a coincidence. He had wanted to find a spot as far from Katie's aunt, Mattie Baxter, as possible, and Wicklow, in addition, had the reputation of being a place where an Irishman could be himself. There was another more secret, more sinister, reason, too. O'Brien's brother Dermot was deeply involved in terrorist activities in Britain, and although he was always careful not to upset his own applecart, O'Brien gathered a little money from sympathisers in the district, and sent it away to help the Cause.

When Katie was about four months pregnant, Wesley went away on one of his mysterious trips to Melbourne, and left his wife in charge, with a little hired assistance from Adolphus Fisher. The lonely girl, like Harry Radford, found the view from the dunes across the tossing waters to the island quite fascinating, and when she could snatch an hour from her drudgery, she enjoyed a walk on the beach. There was a way, she had discovered, to cross the river when the water was low, provided that she did not mind wetting her feet. Sand had built up against a ridge of rock, and it was here that, in years gone by, the native blacks had placed their fish traps. It was a short cut, for the more conventional way to reach the beach was to walk half a mile along the track to Garranbete, cross the bridge built of logs placed across several beams and then packed with dirt, and virtually double back towards the shore.

For September, the day had been unusually warm, after several dry weeks, so that the river was lower than usual for that time of the year. For once, Katie felt almost lighthearted, and decided that there was nothing to be done which could not wait. She cut herself a lunch, and called out to 'Dolly', who was repairing a fence, that she was going for a walk. It was an effort to toil up over the dunes, and for the first time she understood the limitations of pregnancy. Still, out of breath though she was, she stood on top of the last dune, exhilarated by the view across the sea to the flat-topped island. There used to be seals on the island, 'Dolly' had told her, until the hunters had clubbed most of them for their skins and oil. That was a long time ago, when his father was a young man, and his mother, kidnapped from Tasmania, had helped with the capture and killing of the animals. Between times, they lived near where Warnambool had since been built, boiling down the carcasses for oil, and growing a few vegetables in the rich black soil. Then one day, other white men had arrived, legal settlers, and eventually, a clergyman, who had talked severely to 'Dolly's' father about the poor black woman he held in bondage. From force of habit, Fisher Senior had become fond of the savage creature who had shared so much of his life, and after a great deal of grumbling, had married her legally, and had his small tribe of offspring baptised. Until the day she died, said 'Dolly' who was a great talker when he had an audience, Mrs Fisher used to go to the beach and gaze across the water towards Tasmania, nearly two hundred miles away, and cry out of homesickness. But, even when she had the chance, she would not go back. They treated black people too badly there, she said.

Katie did not feel sad looking out across the sea. She was, after all, still in her teens, and today, with Wesley away and the sun shining so brightly, she yielded to an impulse and, sitting herself down, slid herself on to the beach by pushing at the sand with her hands. It was great fun, and afterwards she sat on the beach, eating her bread and cheese, skirts hitched up so that her feet and calves were toasted gently by the sun.

Then she went for a walk along the water's edge, watching out for large shells. She had found several big ones about here, unbroken, and they now decorated the shelf over the fireplace.

Katie, absorbed in this gentle pastime, was startled out of her contentment by the sound of hoofbeats thudding along the beach, and she turned, afraid of whom might be riding towards her. Women, she knew, always took a risk in going alone to isolated places, and she began hurrying back towards the dunes.

'Katie.'

The horseman pulled up his mount, and called after her, as she began her scrambling ascent. It was Conan O'Brien.

'Don't run away,' he added.

He was riding a sprightly little bay mare, not very well, for he had only recently taken up the practice. She hesitated, and returned to the flat sand. He dismounted, and smiled at her, although secretly he was shocked at her shabby appearance. Her dress was threadbare to an extreme, and could have afforded little warmth on the chilly days which were a general rule at this time of year, while the boots she carried were all but worn out. Still, her face was well scrubbed, and her complexion fresher than he remembered it.

'Hullo, Con,' she whispered, shyly, not looking at him directly.

'What are you doing here on your own?'

'Wes is away, and I like walking on the beach.'

'If you had an accident, no one'd ever find you. Still, let's walk together for a bit.'

That was the start of it. She did not see him again for two weeks, when she passed him in the street whilst shopping in Wicklow, and the rush of longing within her was startling. This was the man who should have been her husband, who had worried so much about her wretched life with Aunt Mattie. Their secret meetings were infrequent, but sweet for all that, and about the time that the news of Prince Alfred's arrival in Australia became current, O'Brien began talking seriously about the chances of their leaving Victoria together and starting up a new life together, somewhere else.

At first, Katie found it hard to agree. In spite of everything, she was a firm believer in the sanctity of marriage vows. Another factor, unexpressed, but real enough, was the chance that Con would tire of her, and without marriage lines to bind them, why should he stay with her? And there was the baby, of which her husband was actually very fond. Would Con always treat poor little Maria as his own daughter?

Eventually, Wesley found out about her meetings with Conan O'Brien, and he thrashed her until she lay sobbing and almost senseless upon the beaten earth floor of their shack. The next day, he forced her to accompany him into Wicklow, so that she had to show her bruised face to all the curious townspeople, and worst of all, Con. There had been the beginnings of a stand-up fight, but Constable Evans and Mr Radford had put a stop to it. Poor Katie felt that she had really reached the ultimate depths of shame and misery when she saw the pity in Mr Radford's eyes. Unlike her husband, she had neither hatred nor envy for the Radfords, and she admired Mrs Harry Radford, to whom she had never spoken, although Mrs Radford had sent over some baby clothes when Maria was born. To Katie, Helena was the epitome both in elegance and kindness, the sort of person one gaped at in quiet adoration from afar.

For a while, Wesley kept a very close watch upon her. He did not want her for himself, but she was, after all, his property, a useful worker, and necessary for the wellbeing of his child. However, it is quite extraordinary what parted and desperate lovers can do under the most difficult circumstances. A note found its way to Con O'Brien telling him that Wesley was off to Melbourne on one of his business trips. (The debts had piled up again, and although Wesley actually toyed with the idea of taking his wife and child with him this time, he decided against it in the end. Instead he settled down to scaring the wits out of Katie so that she would behave herself during his absence.)

Wesley was no sooner past Wicklow on his

way to Melbourne than Con was at the Eggert shack, and Katie, sobbing, was in his arms.

'Dear love, don't cry.' Con kissed and caressed her until she quietened. 'Now listen to me, carefully. I've sold the pub. Kept it very quiet. I arranged it all through an agent up in Melbourne. We'll be away together before Wes gets back.'

'What about the fowls and the cows?' Katie, with little other company, had made friends with the domestic livestock, and their welfare was of very real concern to her.

'I'll pay "Dolly" Fisher to come over and look after them.'

Katie, who wanted nothing more than to leave her unhappiness behind and start a new life with her lover, demurred.

'I'll miss seeing Prince Alfred,' she said.

It mattered enormously to her. Seeing a son of the great Queen Victoria, right here on the track going past the Eggert farm, in the flesh, was an experience akin to a miracle. She wanted to hold up little Maria so that when the child grew older, she could say, 'When you were a baby, you saw Prince Alfred, the son of the Queen, and he looked at you.'

Even after they had made love, taking their

time because there was no imminent danger of discovery, Katie came back to the subject of the prince.

'If we don't see him in Wicklow, we'll catch up with him somewhere else. Sydney or Brisbane perhaps,' promised Conan, pulling on his shirt as Katie languidly watched him from the bed. 'I daresay that's one reason Wes went up to Melbourne. To see Prince Alfred. Now, dear heart, when the time is right, I'll send for you, and you must come. Do you understand?'

'It will be before Wes gets back?' Her nervous brown eyes implored him to reassure her. She was quite at the end of her tether as far as Eggert was concerned, and ready to bolt whether or not Con took her.

'Of course. We'll be away two days before the Prince comes. Funny Wes didn't wait until he'd been and gone. Still, from what I heard, he needed this money he goes up to Melbourne to get pretty badly.' He sat down on the edge of the bed, and stroked Katie's tumbled hair, gently. 'He's a queer bird, all right. Anyone else 'd have their money sent along through a bank, not go and get it like that.'

'Well, he's got to go to Melbourne for it.'

Now O'Brien became curious. He had heard rumours about Eggert's source of income, reputedly from an investment Katie's husband had made some years before after a lucky strike at the goldfields.

Katie was suddenly evasive. Wesley had always treated her like dirt, but there was a point of betrayal beyond which she would not go.

'I don't know,' she mumbled. 'The baby's crying, Con.'

Before he left, O'Brien again emphasised that they would be going away two days before Prince Alfred arrived, as soon as the change over of the Rose of Tralee was completed, and the new owner had checked through the inventory. With all the fuss and bother of the Prince's coming, people would hardly notice that they were leaving together. It was all working out wonderfully well. By the time Wesley Eggert realised what had happened, they would be so far away that he could never catch up with them.

Katie was still disappointed that they would miss seeing His Royal Highness on his way to the Radfords' picnic, for he would be passing within two hundred yards of the shack. There would be no one else waiting. She would be able to stand there and wave, and he could not miss seeing her, and he would perhaps wave back, and, impossible dream, stop his coach and say a few words to the baby. It was the sort of thing which would be the highlight of an entire lifetime for a person like Katie, but sadly, she gave up the chance. To her, obedience came naturally, and now that she had decided to throw in her lot with Con, it was only right that she should defer to his superior wisdom.

For O'Brien, everything was working out splendidly. He was assisting the Fenian cause and avenging a brother by ensuring that the Eggert farmhouse would be deserted while Stephen Doyle awaited Prince Alfred. At the same time, he was taking away the girl who should have been his in the first place, thus paying back Wesley Eggert.

Prince Alfred would be dead, Conan O'Brien would be so far away that no one would suspect his part in the plot, and Major Doyle, aided by a good horse, should escape quite easily back to Warnambool, where he would be concealed by a sympathiser until he could be smuggled away on a ship.

It would, thought Con, go like clockwork. The weakness of clockwork, of course, is that so little is needed to put it out of order.

Fifteen

Harry Radford was not a man for dramatic scenes. There was too much of the stolid English countryman in his makeup for that. He and Helena dined together as usual, and although she was pale and silent, eating little, he uttered the usual commonplaces about the day's events on the run. This must have been for the benefit of the servants, for immediately after the meal, he excused himself, saying that he had letters to write. She was undressed for the night, and had dismissed Miss McPherson before the moment came.

He walked briskly into the big, airy bedroom on the first floor which they shared, for they followed the Australian custom of one bedroom for master and mistress together, whatever the status of the household.

'Well, Lena,' he said, 'I've written to Mr

Revell in Melbourne.'

Mr Revell was the lawyer who handled most of Harry Radford's legal business, and the unexpected mention of his name told Helena just what her husband had in mind for her. Dismissal.

'You can leave the morning of the day after we entertain the Prince. That gives you another full two days here.'

Then he turned to leave, but she could not let him.

'Harry,' she implored, running forward and taking his arm, 'you haven't even asked me whether – whether…' Her voice trailed off as she saw the stoniness of his face.

'I heard enough this afternoon, Lena. And your expression gave you away. You – you cheat.'

'Listen to me.' She would not release her hold on his arm, although he was trying to jerk away, as if he could not bear her touch. 'I was out of my mind with worry. I didn't know what to do. The day you found me by the pond I was plucking up the courage to drown myself. Please, please, Harry, try to understand. I love you, Harry. I have always, almost from the very first.'

'You were planning to make another man's bastard the heir to Garranbete. I gave my youth to this place, Lena. I slaved, and lived in the roughest conditions and ate the roughest food, and yes, by God, did things I'm ashamed to think of now, all for Garranbete.'

'Like fathering Colleen.'

The instant the bitter words were out, she knew that she had made the worst mistake of all.

'Colleen's mother was not my wife, and she knew that she would never be my wife. There's nothing more to be said. I want you to be out of my house – and my life – as soon as decently possible.'

For Helena, that sleepless night spent alone in the wide brass bed normally shared with her husband, seemed endless. Her emotions were a mixture of shock and amazement, for in a few hours, the whole fabric of her life had been ripped apart. She was the one at fault. There was no escaping that. She had acted with a stupidity which seemed incredible to her now, a few years later. She had allowed herself to be seduced like any vulgar servant girl. How could she explain it to Harry when she could not understand it herself?

All she knew was that Andrew had appeared during a phase in her life when hopelessness had bowed her down, when it was an effort to drag herself from her bed of a morning, and the days stretched ahead of her in an endless grey procession. To share little jokes, kisses, and later, intimate embraces, which brought her a joy beyond her imagining, had been an escape from the reality which was making her existence a burden.

Then or now, there was no one to tell Helena that she had fallen a victim to that strange malady, melancholia, later to be called depression, brought about by the twin pressures of the shock of her fiance's death and the frustrations of her life.

There was something ironic in the way Ailsa had thought she had found a choice little titbit to wield as a weapon to cut Helena down to size. Ailsa had, Helena was sure, absolutely no idea of the real truth. Ailsa had never made any secret of the fact that she thought Colleen's existence a disgrace on the family name. To discover that Harry had been trapped into marriage gave her a lot of satisfaction.

Towards dawn, Helena slept a little after crying for hours, and then awoke to the familiar sound of the laughing jackass in the old gum tree which had been allowed to remain in the front garden. She and Harry had had many mild arguments about that same tree. She detested its peeling bark and dropping leaves, not soft and quick to decay like those leaves with which she was more familiar, but tough and apt to lie about for a long time. Harry said that the tree had to remain because the laughing jacks favoured it. She liked the birds with their odd calls, so like peals of human laughter, but thought that they could have found another tree.

A difference of opinion over a tree seemed very trivial as Helena pushed aside the covers restlessly, for the day had dawned warm and sultry.

He had, she discovered, left the house at half an hour past dawn to ride to a more distant part of the run where wild dogs had attacked some sheep. Her own day would be full enough. The cooked meats for the morrow had to be prepared, tarts and cakes made, and every effort expended to see that nothing could happen to mar the picnic.

The servants, of course, knew that something had happened between the master and mistress. Blankets strewn from the sofa in the room he used as a study advertised that, and Helena was conscious of the housemaid's sly glances as she hurried past with the folded blankets in her arms. At the same time, Helena could not help wondering why Harry had not asked that a bed be made up in one of the other bedrooms. They were not short of sleeping accommodation, but she sensed that he was making it plain that things in this house would not be set to rights until she left.

What would she do? As she tried to eat some breakfast, the question thumped inside her aching head. She had gathered from what Harry had said that arrangements would be made for an allowance. She knew next to nothing about the grounds for legal separation, and less than nothing about that extraordinary modern innovation, divorce. She could not imagine Harry attempting to obtain the latter, with every particular being relished by every reader of the scurrilous scandal sheets. She wanted to weep into her cup of tea.

Life had to go on, and giving up the effort of forcing down food, she went out to the kitchen, and discussed the preparations for the picnic. It was tacit that a good front must still be presented on the following day: Helena's little world had collapsed, but the facade had to be preserved for another forty-eight hours.

As she entered the kitchen, a woman who had come over from Wicklow was imparting what passed for sensational news in that dull hamlet. Mr O'Brien had sold up the Rose of Tralee, and no one had even guessed that such a thing had happened until the new owner had arrived yesterday.

You'll have something more interesting to talk about in a few days' time, thought Helena.

It was while she was crossing the wide entrance hall to the foot of the staircase that Helena remembered Harry's letter to Revell. The letter could not have gone out of the house yet. There was a custom here at Garranbete that all letters intended for mailing were left on a salver placed on a small table near the front door. When the mailman made his twice-weekly visit, he would collect the outgoing correspondence, which included that of the servants and others employed at Garranbete as well as any being dispatched by Mr and Mrs Radford. This was his day.

For the moment, Helena was alone in this part of the house, and on an impulse, she quickly rifled through the letters awaiting collection. Mr Revell's was nearly at the

212

bottom, almost as if Harry had deliberately placed it thus, so that it would remain unseen.

Perhaps Harry will have second thoughts. Perhaps he will relent sufficiently to at least talk things over with me. Perhaps if the letter is delayed for a few days...

She picked it up and thrust it into the pocket of her plain cotton dress, starting guiltily as someone spoke to her. It was the cook.

'Mrs Radford, excuse me, but that fellow Fisher is outside the back door. I think he wants to see you, but you know what he's like, Mrs Radford.'

Helena sighed. She indeed knew what 'Dolly' Fisher was like, poor simple minded man.

'It's something about the Eggerts, Mrs Radford, but honestly, I've my hands full at the moment what with...'

'All right. I'll see to it.'

Fisher waited about twenty feet from the back door. He was too shy to come closer to the grandeur of the new Radford house, even at the rear, and when Helena walked out towards him, he lowered his eyes bashfully.

'Now, Mr Fisher,' she said, kindly, 'what is

the trouble?'

'Dolly' was dressed neatly in clean workingman's clothes, that is, fawn moleskin trousers, heavy boots, and a cotton shirt worn under an unbuttoned waistcoat. He carried his hat in his left hand, and a sugar bag tied halfway down with string rested on the ground near his feet. This last no doubt contained such necessities as a billycan for brewing up tea and food to carry him through the day.

'Well, it's like this, Mrs Radford. I promised Mr Radford about them thistles near the Emu waterhole. Two weeks ago it was, Mr Radford spoke to me about it. "Now," he said to me, in Wicklow it was, "you come about two days before Prince Alfred, remember, so's the thistles 'll be flat if His Royal Highness passes that way." There's a lot of black snakes in them thistles, Mrs Radford. It's near the waterhole, and snakes like to be near water, you see. I'd 'a' come yesterday, but I'd promised to help Mr O'Brien move some stuff.'

Helena nodded patiently. Experience had taught her that one took one's time with Fisher. He always came to the point – eventually.

'Now, Mrs Radford, someone in Wicklow,

and I can't say the name because he asked me not to, told me to drop by the Eggert place today and see that the stock was all right, gettin' water and so on. And I said to this person – can't mention the name, Mrs Radford – that's funny. Mr Eggert didn't ask me to do that this time. Mrs Eggert is there and she manages all right if Mr Eggert isn't there or when Mr Eggert isn't himself. Since I signed the pledge, Mrs Radford, I've spoken to Mr Eggert about the drink, but 'e tells me I'm a fool. But I know what's right and wrong, Mrs Radford. Strong drink is ruin, Mrs Radford.'

The sun was up past the roof of the house, and Helena wished that she had brought a hat out with her. Gently, she steered 'Dolly' from what threatened to become a lecture upon the evils of alcohol.

'You stopped at the Eggert place to see to the stock, then?'

'Yes, Mrs Radford. Like I said, this person asked me as a special favour, and gave me five shillings. And I thought, well, if he wants to give me five shillings, that's all right. I need new boots.'

Helena nodded encouragingly, and he continued.

'So, this morning I ups before dawn and

gets a lift with Steve Meagher on the mail cart. He turns off halfway to Eggert's place, you know.'

'Yes, I know, Mr Fisher.' The mailman travelled in a wide circle, passing by Garranbete some time before noon.

'Then I walks the rest of the way, and as I gets near, I thinks, that's funny. She hasn't lit the fire this morning. How's she going to cook up breakfast if she hasn't lit the fire. So I thought, perhaps she's sick and that's why the person – can't mention his name, Mrs Radford – wanted me to look at the stock, Mr Eggert being off to Melbourne.'

'You mean that Mrs Eggert is ill and alone with her baby?'

'No, Mrs Radford. There wasn't nobody there I could make hear. Place was all closed up. But the baby was crying.'

'Didn't you try to get into the house if you were so worried?'

'Oh, no, Mrs Radford. I wouldn't ever do that. If a place is closed up, that means you can't go in. But the baby was crying inside.'

You stupid fool, thought Helena angrily. You – oh, what was the use? 'Dolly' Fisher's mind did not function properly, and that was that.

'I don't know nothing about babies, Mrs Radford. Not to look after them like. That's why I came to tell you on the way to the thistles. I must do the thistles, Mrs Radford. I promised Mr Radford.'

'Yes, of course, Mr Fisher. I'll see to it that something is done.'

Fisher was suddenly all smiles, picking up his bag, and replacing his hat. The responsibility, his jaunty walk seemed to say, as he marched off quickly, had been shifted to more capable shoulders than his own.

Helena quickly sorted through a short list of persons she could send to the Eggert farm. Everyone was extremely busy today, both household and outdoor staff, and even the two Chinese gardeners were away at the river's edge mowing the grass and turning a piece of ordinary bushland into what Harry Radford hoped would be a sylvan glade. She decided to go herself. Quite obviously, Mrs Eggert was too sick to attend to the baby, or even come out to tell 'Dolly' Fisher that she needed help. Just as obviously, a woman's assistance was preferable to that of a man.

Within ten minutes, Helena, glad to have something besides her own troubles to occupy her mind, had changed into her summer riding habit, and was mounted on her mare, Felicity.

She rode across country, glad to be free of the house, and as she left Garranbete behind her, smelling the fresh breeze off the ocean. The Eggert farm, she thought, must be a cold, dank place in winter, with the perpetual winds blowing off the sea, and the water gathering in the low places. And, she noticed, as Felicity crossed the track and trotted along the rutted way through the thickets which separated the Eggert property from the rest of the world, the sand was creeping inland. Wesley Eggert had cleared some of the land immediately behind the dunes by burning the dense vegetation, and now, without that growth to act as a bulwark, the sand was sliding hungrily inland.

The farm itself was a ramshackle collection of buildings, set out more or less in a row, with the largest, a barn, to Helena's right as she approached. The homestead, identified by its chimney, stood about thirty yards to the left of the barn, its front door opening towards the paddocks which rambled away to the river flowing behind the dunes. On the other side of the house was a motley gathering of small outhouses, crudely constructed from split palings as the need for them arose. A few hens scratched about the yard, two milch cows chewed at baled hay in an enclosure of their own, and Eggert's few cattle were scattered across the paddocks.

As Fisher had told Helena, the chimney was smokeless, and there was all about an air of great loneliness, and an almost eerie silence, interrupted only by the harsh sounds of some crows gathered together in a dead tree about a hundred yards distant. There's no one here, she thought. 'Dolly' imagined it all.

She drew rein, intending to turn her horse about and ride away. It was then she heard, faintly, a baby's cry. It was enough. She rode into the flattened bare space separating the barn from the house, and dismounted. Felicity whinnied, and almost straight away there was an answering sound from the barn.

That settles it, she thought. The Eggerts cannot be away from home. Their wretched old horse is still here.

She went to the barn and looked inside. What she saw was not the Eggert's tired old beast, an animal which had spent its life as a jack-of-all-trades, but a smart brown gelding with a white blaze on its forehead.

There was so much which was wrong here. The horse, the smokeless chimney, the baby's cry, the lack of washing on the clothesline. And no dog. That was why it was so quiet. Every farmhouse had a dog, to help the farmer and guard a woman on her own in an isolated homestead.

Helena conquered her rising unease, and hitched Felicity to a post before walking across to the house, brushing away a myriad of flies as she did so.

Sixteen

'You must go away.' The words were uttered in a sibilant whisper which stopped Helena in midstep.

Mrs Eggert was outside the front door of the shack, untidy and wild-eyed, her left hand held out in a gesture at once warning and commanding.

'Is there something wrong? Is the baby sick? Mr Fisher said that...'

'Please go. Quickly. There's nothing wrong.'

Yet, at the same time, Helena knew that

220

Katie Eggert was trying to tell her something else. She was pointing back towards
the door with her other hand, held low in
front of her grubby skirt, and at the same
time shaking her head.

'All right. If you are sure I cannot help.'

Katie Eggert's face was starkly white, her
dark eyes almost sunken, and her small
frame tense. She showed every sign of being
in an extreme of terror.

Helena turned on her heel, returned to
Felicity, and unhitched the mare.

'Could you give me a step up, do you
think?' she asked, turning suddenly to catch
a glimpse of movement in the doorway
behind Katie.

'I– I– yes, of course, Mrs Radford.'

The younger woman ran forward, and
Helena asked her quickly, in a very low
voice, whether she should fetch help.

'No. Nothing's wrong. Nothing. Just go.'

Mounted, Helena looked down at Katie
Eggert, seeing the swelling on one side of
her jaw and the tell-tale bruising on her
forearm, revealed by the sleeve which had
been rolled up to the elbow. So, this was
another domestic fracas, of the kind about
which Harry had already warned Eggert. To
interfere would most likely bring fresh

repercussions to be suffered by poor Katie.

By the time she had reached the road, Helena knew that she could not let the matter rest. Something *was* wrong, and no man had the right to reduce his wife to such a pitiful state. So, again she dismounted, and led Felicity into the extensive shelter of the strip of virgin bush, about two chains in depth, which ran alongside the road here. Part of this natural plantation was on Eggert's land; the rest on public land which had been left for road widening when the surveyors had been through. It was almost the last stand of the original forest which had once spread across much of the land which now belonged to Harry Radford. Some of this forest had been cleared by the endeavours of the Radford brothers and their team of convict workers, but most had vanished, literally in a puff of smoke, on a hellish day back in 1851, when one of the largest fires in history had raged through much of what was then called the Port Phillip District. This scrap, bordering the Eggert land, had been spared, and within its confines stood a few large and aged trees, surrounded by almost hedge-like stands of wattle, paperbarks, and the parasitic native cherry. Helena tied Felicity to a sapling, and edged cautiously from this cover back towards the Eggert farmhouse.

She had no very clear idea of what she intended to do. Perhaps, if she had the chance, she could persuade Mrs Eggert to bring herself and her baby back to Garranbete.

She reached the barn without being seen, as far as she could calculate, and hesitated, not knowing what to do next. She was starting to think that she was making a fool of herself when Katie came out from the shack, carrying a bucket, and making for the pump. Everything seemed so very normal now. There was a little smoke coming from the chimney, indicating some kind of domestic activity, and in the barn, a hen cackled madly, telling the world that she had produced an egg.

Katie saw her, and despite Helena's raising of a warning finger to her lips, yelped and dropped the bucket. Almost immediately, a man came out of the shack, and Helena stared at him in astonishment.

It was not Wesley Eggert, but the red-headed Yankee stove salesman.

Stephen Doyle anticipated a full day and several hours at the Eggert's farm. A preliminary inspection of the country thereabouts had helped him to formulate his final plan. At first, he had intended to shoot Prince Alfred from the cover of the thick bush by the road, but when he discovered that the royal visitor would be making his travels through the Western District in a coach provided by the famous transport company, Cobb and Co, he changed his mind. There were too many 'ifs and buts'. A party of men could manage it, by shooting the driver and forcing the inside passengers to leave the shelter of the coach, but for a single man the task was virtually impossible.

After his first interview with Conan O'Brien, he had scouted out the land almost to the Garranbete homestead itself, remaining on the far side of the river, and easily identifying the fenced-off enclosure where the picnic was to take place. Here, the young Prince would be relaxed and moving about freely, and a band of trees left as a windbreak would provide Doyle with cover until the right moment came. The worst part of it would be reaching his horse, left downstream, but he counted on complete confusion to give him the start he needed. The terrain could not have been better, slightly rolling, but with no real obstacle between him and escape. By the time his would-be pursuers had mounted up, he would be miles away.

The chance to rest up quietly at the Eggert farm for a day was a tremendous stroke of luck. His horse would be rested, he would have the opportunity to shave off his beard, and extra time to explore the locality.

O'Brien warned him about the half-caste, Fisher. (Major Doyle thought of the part-Tasmanian as a halfbreed, American style.) There was an arrangement, O'Brien said, whereby Fisher checked on the Eggerts' stock when they were away, milking their couple of cows, making sure the hens were fed, and that there were no wild dogs about, and so on. He would most likely be turning up early in the day, and again just before dusk, as he had a job to do for the Radfords, cutting down Scotch thistles, on the day before Prince Alfred was expected. As one of Wicklow's two publicans, O'Brien knew all the trivia of local gossip, and was invaluable to Stephen Doyle.

'You're quite sure the place will be deserted?' Doyle still had this niggling, nagging feeling that everything was too good to be true.

Conan O'Brien repeated his assurance. Eggert was off to Melbourne, and the wife would be away too. He knew that for a fact, and as long as Sam Doherty watched out for 'Dolly' Fisher, he should remain undetected.

The well-wisher at Warnambool not only promised aid in leaving the country. He was a close friend of one of those Irishmen serving out their time as political prisoners in Western Australia, which still accepted convicts from the United Kingdom. As well as assuring Doyle (whom he knew only as Sam Doherty) that he would see him safely on his way to Sydney by sea, and from thence to California, he provided an excellent horse.

So Doyle rode back from the port towards Wicklow and Garranbete in leisurely style. This time, he avoided the Rose of Tralee and Wicklow, camping out, no hardship on a warm, dry night. In the morning, he rode along the beach, which was quite deserted, and then up through the sandhills towards Eggert's farm. He paused on the last dunes, looking across the river and the patchily cleared paddocks to the cluster of greyish small buildings, assuring himself that the farm was indeed deserted, and that no smoke was coming from the chimney although dawn was two hours past.

Rather than risk his horse on the unknown quantity of the river, which he would check during that day of planning and exploration, he skirted Eggert's three hundred acres, and crossed the river by the bridge at the point where the road divided into that going westwards and the smaller track turning north to Garranbete. Riding back towards Eggert's farm, he saw, in the distance, the skinny, energetic figure of Fisher, whom he had had pointed out to him in Wicklow by O'Brien. 'Dolly' did not bother with the road, but, carrying his bundle, set off briskly across country, toward Garranbete homestead. Doyle knew that the half-caste was a little simple, and did not anticipate much bother in avoiding him.

A few hens still pecked busily at an old dish containing the remnants of the mash set out for them by Fisher. They roamed free during the day, being kept, not always successfully, from the small vegetable patch by a roughly latticed fence. A pig grunted in its pen nearby, and the two milch cows had been let loose into a paddock. This farm, he thought, was one of the poorest he had ever seen, with not much to choose between it and those of the wretched poor white farmers of the Southern States, despised by plantation owners and slaves alike. He wondered how anyone could make even a pretence of a decent living from the place as he led his horse into the barn and unsaddled the animal.

He took a bucket and pumped up water from the well in the yard, attending, from the force of habit brought about by his years in the army, to the wants of his mount first. He would, he thought, leave some money for the chaff he took. He was, after all, a patriot, not a thief.

Carrying a small bundle of necessities which he had brought with him, and that other bundle, the most important, he walked casually across to the shack which was home to the Eggerts. He would have liked a cup of tea, or better, some coffee, but lighting a fire could be too risky, so that he would have to make do with plain water today. The door, as O'Brien had promised, was not locked, and pushed open at a touch.

A slight young woman with untidy brown hair and scared brown eyes stared at him as she sat huddled on a three-legged stool near the open fireplace, which contained only the dead ashes from yesterday.

He felt the shock of betrayal. She must be, could only be, Mrs Eggert. But what was she doing here? And she looked scared out of her wits.

'I'm sorry,' he said, thinking quickly. 'I was told Mr Eggert would be here.'

'Mr Eggert's in Melbourne.' The words came out in a sort of stammered whisper. 'You're Mr Doherty, aren't you?'

Now, what was this? His nerve ends warned him to leave immediately, but at the same time, ordinary common sense told him that he must act in a matter of fact fashion. He silently called down a million curses on Con O'Brien's head.

'At your service, ma'am.' He put down his bundles, and swept his hat from his head, making a bow, with all the best of American courtesy. 'I'm sorry I startled you, but I understood...'

By all the saints, what was he to do now?

'Con told me you'd be coming.' She spoke in a monotone scarcely above a whisper, but his ear caught the flat, nasal inflection of the native-born Australian.

'Then, you're Mrs Eggert?'

He made his own voice sound kindly,

whilst trying to suppress his impatience and disappointment.

'Yes. I'm Katie Eggert.'

A baby commenced crying somewhere near at hand, and he saw for the first time an infant lying in a crib in a sort of lean-to annexe opening off this room which served both as kitchen and general living-room. She looked at him in that shrinking, yet strangely dull, way of hers, and then went to the child, picking it up, and hugging it against her.

'Katie? Is that Irish?'

'I dunno. Perhaps. My name's really Katherine, but no one's ever called me that.'

'Well, Katherine, what did Mr O'Brien tell you about me?'

She half turned towards him, her face blank and stupid. He noticed now that she had moved into better light that there was a contusion on one side of her jaw.

'Nothing,' said Katie. 'Just nothing. He told me – told me – your name's Mr Doherty. That's all.'

She was scared. Her small frame screamed it out, by the jerkiness of her movements, the damp pallor of her skin, and the curious opaqueness of her eyes. He had seen young men like that, as they went

230

into their first battle.

'Then you expected me, Katherine.' He deliberately used the whole form of her name. He guessed that few persons had ever honoured this drab and wretched girl in that way before, and he wanted to soothe her, to calm her, as one would a frightened animal. She was here. She had been warned of his coming. And perhaps Con knew what he was doing. In any case, she could light the fire and make him a cup of tea, and prepare some cooked food.

She nodded, dumbly.

'There's nothing to be afraid of,' he said, hastily revising his plans inside his head. 'I'll be gone by noon. I'm on my way to Portland.'

Portland was the westerly settlement towards the South Australian border. He would have to head in that direction and hide in the scrub somewhere until tomorrow morning.

'All right.' Her acceptance of his presence puzzled him. Was this all a trap? Ireland, he knew too well, had produced as many traitors as heroes.

'Who hit you?' he asked, taking her by surprise. She had put the baby down again, and now moved to a dresser, taking a bowl off a shelf, perhaps with the intention of mixing up some food for the child. The bowl shook in her trembling fingers, and she put it down hastily on the scrubbed top of the deal table.

'Hit me?' Her eyes lost their dullness, and darted from side to side, as if seeking an escape.

He began to wonder if, like 'Dolly' Fisher, she was lacking in the head.

'Yes. There's a mark on your jaw.'

'I – I fell. In the dark. The baby cried and I got up, and I fell.'

'Could you make me some tea? I don't expect you have coffee?'

'Only tea.'

'Attend to the baby first. Could I start the fire for you?'

The simple offer paralysed her. She stood as if stricken for several moments, her lips moving, but no words coming.

'No. Don't. Not yet. It's too hot. The place gets too hot if the fire's going all the time.'

'All right.'

The baby was yelling again, and he thought, of course, the girl's embarrassed. She doesn't want to unbutton her blouse in front of a stranger. Above all, he wanted to leave a good impression, so that if they asked her tomorrow about any strangers she had seen, she could tell them about the kindly and polite caller who was travelling across to Portland.

'I'll go out and see if my horse is all right. I left it in the barn.'

'Why did you put it there?'

'Well, it's hot in the sun, and there isn't much other shelter,' he replied. 'I'll leave you to your child.'

Out in the barn, he crouched down and unrolled that second bundle, a heavy piece of canvas, divided into slots and pockets. He assembled his rifle. If he had been betrayed, he would not give in without a fight. And he wanted a rifle to help build up his story. A great satisfaction passed through him as he finished his task. There was a weapon. If the Union troops had had this rifle, the war would have been over in six months. He had heard of the Australian bushrangers, Hall and Gardiner, who only a few years since had terrorised outback New South Wales, and had become folk heroes in songs popular at the lower type of Australian music hall. With Winchesters in their saddle holsters, they would be roaming still.

This was the best gun ever created, and he wondered if there was, at this time, another specimen in the whole of Australia. Not only was it uncannily accurate, but enough bullets to kill a royal prince and all his entourage could be pumped out through its barrel at a long range without a pause to reload. He held success in his hands, if only he could trust O'Brien, who for some inexplicable reason, had involved that slow-witted girl in the shack.

He carried the gun back to the shack, and Katie, wiping the baby's face with a damp cloth, gasped. This simpleton would not know one gun from another, he thought, scornfully.

'Don't be frightened. I'm hoping to shoot a few kangaroos this afternoon.'

He propped the unloaded weapon against the wall, feeling more confident now that ammunition weighed down the pockets of his jacket.

'You'd better fetch some water,' he added, when she had placed the baby back in her crib. 'The bucket seems to be empty.'

Then he felt ashamed of himself.

'No, don't worry,' he amended. 'I'll do it. You get the fire going.'

It was at this instant that they both heard a horse approaching. He was at the window in a trice, pushing aside the hessian hanging which doubled as curtain and blind, and peering out. There was one horse, and the rider, he saw immediately, was a woman, although he did not recognise her, for her hat partly screened her face as she looked about. To his alarm, she alighted and walked across to the barn, glanced in, and turned to stare at the shack before coming towards it.

'Who is it?' he hissed at Katie.

'It's – it's Mrs Radford.'

He knew the name well enough. It was imprinted into his mind along with the clearing by the river, the picnic lunch, and Prince Alfred.

'Friend of yours?' He kept his voice low whilst his brain churned about seeking a solution.

Katie shook her head, dumbly, and he could see that her bewilderment was genuine.

'All right then. You wouldn't want her to know you've a man here with Mr Eggert away, would you? Get rid of her. Don't let her inside.' As he concluded, he patted her shoulder, in a friendly, encouraging and brotherly sort of way. Obediently, she went outside.

Damnation. What was the woman doing here? Con had told him that there was a feud between the Eggerts and the Radfords. Well, fingers crossed, and faith in the angels that this stupid girl would have the wits to bluff it out.

For all his misgivings, she seemed to manage very well, although when the visitor called Katie over to assist her in mounting her horse, he held his breath. But Katie made short work of it, and he would have been easy again, except for one thing. For the first time, he saw Mrs Radford's face clearly as she thanked Katie for her assistance.

It was the young woman who had been watching him from the balcony in Ballarat.

Major Doyle felt that familiar prickling in his spine. He had dreamt of priests the previous night, always a bad omen, although he had tried to rationalize it when he awoke by remembering the feeling of guilt he had experienced for not taking the mass whilst he had had the chance in Warnambool. How could a man make his confession with murder on his soul, and on his mind? In some way, this woman, this Mrs Radford, was an evil portent, and when Katie returned indoors, his pretence slipped away. He grabbed her by the arm, fiercely, so that she cried out in pain.

236

'Tell me the truth. Who is she, and why did she come here?'

For the first time, Katie Eggert showed a little fight.

'It was Mrs Radford, like I told you. What's wrong with you? The law's after you, ain't it?'

He let go of her, inwardly cursing himself for giving way to superstitious fear.

'Never mind. Now get that fire going. Make me some tea and I'll be gone within the hour.'

Katie began crying, but she knelt down and cleared away the ashes to one side of the fireplace, and started up a fresh fire with some kindling. Gone was his simple chivalrous intent of pumping up water for her. He was staying here in the shack, rifle to hand.

'You still didn't tell me why she came here nosing about.'

Katie stood up, dusting ashes from her apron.

'She thought I was sick, that's all.'

It seemed likely enough, the kindly act of a neighbour, except that the Radfords and Eggerts were at loggerheads, according to Con O'Brien. But could he trust anything O'Brien had said? Had she perhaps been sent to spy out the lay of the land?

Don't be stupid, he told himself. They wouldn't send the lady of the manor.

He could not rid himself of the acute sensation that there was something actively wrong here, although no logic he could muster was able to identify it.

'You'd better fetch the water,' he ordered.

It was while he watched Katie scurrying towards the pump that he saw Mrs Radford, slim and graceful in her summer riding habit, and manifestly trying to remain unnoticed, as she slipped along the side of the barn.

His reaction was purely reflex. He picked up his rifle and walked out to confront her just as the alarmed Katie Eggert dropped her bucket.

Seventeen

Helena's main emotion, as she stared at the rifle held so casually by the man she knew as Sam Doherty, was one of absolute disbelief.

'Put that thing down,' she commanded, very much mistress of Garranbete.

He laughed.

'No, Mrs Radford, not until you tell me why you're here.'

Helena studied him, apparently very much in control, but sick with fear inside. Why had she come back? Later, she would analyse her reasons, and discover that, right at base, she had wanted a confrontation with Wesley Eggert. She had wanted to lash him with her tongue, to threaten him with the law, and pay him back for all the miseries men inflicted upon womankind. She was not afraid of Wesley Eggert. She saw him as a miserable little bully, brave enough when it came to inflicting pain on a helpless girl, but basically a coward.

Instead, she came out with another reason, true but trivial.

'There was no dog here,' she stated.

For several seconds, Major Doyle just stared at her. Of course. That was it, that was the cause of his unease. Who had ever heard of a farm without a dog?

'Where's the dog?' he asked Katie, who again seemed seized with that curious dull-eyed paralysis.

'It went. It followed Mr Fisher.'

'Go inside, both of you,' he said, after several more moments. Well, everything was in ruins now, thanks to cruel chance and his yielding to his stupid fear of the supernatural. He knew now why Mrs Radford had stared at him that day in Ballarat. She had recognised him. A cold morning in Melbourne, months ago. A big, prosperous, fair man, and this woman, elegant in a fur-trimmed travelling costume. Acting out his part as the brash Yankee, he had ogled her.

The best he could hope for now was to get as far away as possible from this accursed place, and try again in Sydney. He had let himself become rattled, and he had to make the best of things.

With Katie following, Helena walked to the shack, as slowly as she dared, yet not so tardily as to anger her captor. She could only hope that 'Dolly' Fisher had told his story to someone else with the patience to listen, and that someone would have the curiosity to come here to the Eggert farm.

Stepping indoors, she saw the many evidences of the poverty in which a higher proportion of these 'selectors' lived. An earthen floor, walls lined with old newspaper pasted over the boards and then whitewashed, a dividing wall made of hessian and then treated in the same way with old papers and whitewash. No wonder, she thought, irrelevantly, these places go up like torches when they catch fire.

'You're quite out of your mind, you know,' she said, quietly, seating herself on a three-legged stool. Her voice was still level. She was sure that she was dealing with a madman, and that the best chance of escape for herself and Katie was to keep him talking.

Doyle was now studying her more closely. The incident at the hotel came back to him with some clarity. He remembered that he had been a little surprised that she had seemed so disturbed when he had given her 'the eye'. He had expected to be ignored. The remembrance came as a stimulant. She was no evil fairy out of mythology, simply a flesh and blood woman. That was the trouble with being Irish...

He thought that he preferred her in her riding habit, although she was not in looks today, almost as haggard as Mrs Eggert, to be truthful about it. But she was a very lovely woman. There were dark shadows about her eyes; but they were beautiful eyes, soft and mysterious, while her mouth was red and wide, made to be bruised under a man's, and her figure was irreproachable.

Major Doyle was no womanizer, nor was

he the complete ascetic. He felt an intense regret that the meeting had not been under different circumstances, years ago, before this desirable and enchanting woman had become Mrs Radford.

He ignored her comment, but turned to Katie, who had picked up her child, and was holding it to her as if trying to protect the infant.

'Katherine,' he said, 'what is the building on the other side from the barn?'

'The wood shed.' The words came out as if torn from a constricted throat.

'Good. Now give the baby to Mrs Radford, and you go out to the barn and fetch me some rope. I saw some out there.'

'You're serving no purpose by acting like this,' said Helena. 'Someone is going to miss me at home.'

Fool, she thought. When they do miss you, they won't know where you are.

'Never mind that. Do as I say, Katherine.'

Katie handed the baby to Helena, who took it in her arms, and smiled, with a reassurance she certainly did not feel, at the other woman.

'Hurry,' snapped Doyle, and Katie, starting to sob again, obeyed him.

Helena gently jogged the baby up and

down on her lap, gaining a crow of pleasure for her efforts.

'I can't understand,' she said, over Maria's downy head, 'why you are here, and why you are acting in this absurd manner. Aren't you a commercial traveller?'

He did not answer, but his cold eyes did not move from her face, and his rifle, which was actually still unloaded, remained pointed at her.

'This is a law-abiding district, you know. Not like the Wild West of America.'

'Where does the law end and oppression start, Mrs Radford?'

It was the sort of question which had never been asked in any conversation in Helena's world, but before she had the need to puzzle out an answer, Katie returned with a long piece of rope.

If I had any sense, Helena thought, I would have been on the back of that horse, saddled or not, and tried to reach Felicity. But if I had done that, what would this fiend have done to poor Mrs Eggert and this innocent baby?

The baby was quite unaffected by the drama being played out about her, and seemed to be enjoying this intrusion of company into the loneliness of Eggert's shack. She had taken a liking to Helena, and gurgled and laughed happily, breaking off to emit an indignant scream when Katie, following Doyle's orders, picked her up and placed her back in her crib.

'Now, Mrs Radford, I want you to tie Mrs Eggert to the chair. Sit down, Mrs Eggert.'

'No,' said Helena. 'I won't do that. The baby…'

'Look,' said Doyle, 'I'm not going to hurt anyone. But I have to get away. Now, tie her up, and do it properly.'

After another few seconds hesitation, Helena obeyed, dreadfully aware of the rifle barrel only a few feet away. She was, of course, quite ignorant of the fact that the gun was not loaded.

Last night, she thought, I wanted to die. I thought of going to the medicine chest and taking our supply of laudanum in one dose. There was nothing to live for. Yet now, when I could so easily die, I want to live.

'Outside.'

Katie had been tied up to his satisfaction, and he indicated to Helena that he wished her to precede him.

'And what do you propose to do with me?'

This time, Helena could not hide the tremor in her voice.

'Nothing. I'll shut you in the woodshed, and then I'll loosen Mrs Eggert just enough so she can work herself free after a while, and by that time I'll be far enough away not to care.' He grinned. 'I wish we'd met under different circumstances, Mrs Radford.'

'I can't imagine the circumstances.'

'Now, that's no way for a fine looking woman like yourself to be talking.'

He no longer sounded American, but decidedly Irish, and the idea came to her, so fantastic that it had to be immediately dismissed.

'If you'll be so good as to open the door, Mrs Radford.'

Helena unfastened the door of the woodshed, which was kept shut by means of a hook and eye, that is, a small iron loop on the front of the door into which was dropped a large nail, attached to the doorpost by means of a length of rawhide. The door swung outwards on its frayed leather hinges, sagging slightly into the dirt as it did so.

There was wood, cut ready for the fireplace, in that shed. Against the wood leaned an axe, the blade of which was covered with a congealed mass of blood, over which crawled a vast number of black ants. The farm's dog, sliced almost in two, lay beside the body of the master he had failed to defend. There was so much blood that it had not entirely soaked into the dirt and chips of wood and bark, but had instead caked into a layer about the two corpses.

'Holy Mary.' Doyle had seen death so often that he considered that it had long since ceased to affect him, but this gruesome discovery had taken him by surprise. The girl, the wretched young wife, crouching before the fireplace on a stool, terrified out of her wits. Katie Eggert had slaughtered her husband, and he, poor innocent fool, had better look lively or he'd find himself caught for a crime he had not committed.

For Helena, turning away, unable to utter the smallest sound, there could be no doubt. This madman had killed Eggert, and Eggert's dog, and now intended to kill her in like fashion.

She began to run.

'Come back.'

He was too late. She was across the yard, and behind the shelter of the barn. He dodged past the back of the shack and headed her off as she ran towards the road, so that Helena was forced to turn and bolt across the paddocks towards the river, ducking under the sliprails which barred the openings of the roughly fenced enclosures.

Stephen Doyle paused in his stride, loaded his rifle, and fired a shot into the air. His intention at this juncture was to scare her into stopping, so that he could talk with her, and persuade her that he had not murdered Eggert. But Helena kept running, gaining the patchy low scrub near the river, and hoping to be able to double back towards the road, and her tethered horse. He was too quick, and she darted hastily towards the river again as he appeared some fifty yards in front of her.

'Stop, or I'll shoot!'

He fired another shot as she hitched up her skirt and squelched through the shallow water to the opposite bank. There was, she noticed without really absorbing the fact, a sandbar here, and a few ancient stakes, the remnants of an old aboriginal fish trap. Hearing the shot acted as a spur to her efforts, for she was unaware that he had no intention of hitting her. She gained the far bank, and plunged, half bent over, into low scrub, hoping to present less of a target.

The dunes were immediately in front of her, and she could hear the waves beyond.

Instinct rather than sense warned her not to run up on to the sand, for, silhouetted against the white, she must give him the best possible chance of shooting her, and so she struggled on through the scrub, wishing that she could remove her wet boots, crouching to keep as low as possible. The branches scratched her face and hands, prickly growth tore at her clothes, and once a tiger snake slithered across her frantic path. She crawled under a spreading, tangled patch of stunted shrubs, and lay on the littered sand, trying to catch her breath, and praying that he would not see her as he passed.

She was lucky. He crashed past, no more than a yard away, and she pulled off her waterlogged boots. She had hoped that he would think she was still in front of him, but as she crept out to attempt to escape back to the river, and thence, back towards the farm and her horse, he saw her.

'Stop,' he yelled, levelling the rifle. 'This time I will kill you.'

She remembered reading somewhere, in a book belonging to one of the sons of that family with whom she had spent a few happy years, that the thing to do in such circumstances was to run in a zig-zag style.

Fenimore Cooper, that was it, a tale of wild woods and Indians. She blundered a few feet to the right, and then to the left, trying to keep low, and once, flinging herself on to the ground as a bullet whistled past.

She was now dangerously short of breath, and so weary that she was hardly aware of the direction she had taken. Thus, she found herself, without cover, and staggering uphill on loose sand. Somehow, she managed to collect her senses sufficiently to swerve to the right, into the brief protection of a valley between the dunes. She was completely exhausted, and could go no further. With a sigh, she sank to her knees, giving up her soul to God.

It happened so quickly that for several stunned seconds she thought that she had indeed died. One moment, she was lying on the sand, sobbing for breath. The next, she was sliding down into a sort of cave. The contrast between the bright glare of hot sun on white sand, and the shadows of this eerie refuge was so great that for a while she was as if blinded.

Where am I?

Relief began to be superseded by a new terror. She was in some kind of underground cavern, in the dark, trapped.

Huddled in the dark, so tired that further effort was impossible, Helena began to sob, helplessly. So this was the end of the life which, until less than twenty-four hours previously, had been so good and happy.

It's my punishment, she thought, wildly. To die here, alone, slowly, that is my punishment.

Eighteen

For Harry Radford, the watershed in his successful and somewhat complicated life had been reached so unexpectedly that he had not yet grasped the full implications.

His wife, Helena, his darling, dearest Lena, whom he had desired from their first meeting, and whom he had soon come to love deeply, was a common cheat. That was what hurt the most, rather than the discovery that she had not been the chaste creature whom he had placed upon a pedestal. Deliberately, and heartlessly, she had conspired to give his name to a child not his own. He was too blinded by rage and hurt to feel any compassion towards

Helena, who, faced with the worst predicament in which a young woman in her position could find herself, had grasped recklessly at a chance to save her good name and provide for her child.

He certainly did not pause to think that Colleen's feckless mother may have, at one time, felt quite as frightened and alone as Helena must have been. He had, he considered, done the right thing by Colleen's mother.

Harry spent a night quite as sleepless as his wife's. In addition, he had chosen to sleep on a sofa in his office instead of more sensibly in one of the spare bedrooms, and had been uncomfortable as well as miserable. He rode out early, but he found it hard to keep his mind on practical issues. It kept wandering back to that letter he had penned to his lawyer in Melbourne. He had written it in a fury, and now more sober reflection made him doubt the wisdom of his action. Helena had humiliated him, and he wanted to keep it as quiet as possible. Quite a number of English wives decided, after a while, that they disliked the isolation of station life, even on big, wealthy runs such as his. They grew homesick for deciduous trees, the clatter of wheels on paved streets, Yule logs, and all the rest of it, and, on some pretext or another, took themselves back to their homeland.

It would be said that Helena was lonely and homesick, and longed for the more cultured atmosphere of her English background.

Harry decided to ride home quickly and retrieve that letter before the mailman called. The fellow usually came just before noon – Harry suspected that this was a carefully thought out ploy to ensure a good meal, station hospitality being what it was – to leave and collect mail.

So, about eleven, he returned to the homestead. The day was hot, about ninety degrees in the shade, and he was not sorry to dismount and seek the comparative cool of the house, with its thick stone walls and wide verandas. However, a shock awaited him in the hall. The mailman had already been. The letters for collection had gone, and had been replaced by freshly arrived mail, and one or two small packages. In answer to his question, one of the maids told him that Mr Meagher had been early because he was in a hurry to return to Wicklow. Mr Meagher wished to have his hair trimmed because he was playing in the band tomorrow when Prince Alfred passed through Wicklow.

Well, thought Harry, that's that. It's out of my hands now. Even as he accepted this, a fresh wave of anger rushed through him. At this instant in his life, it seemed that everything he had ever done, ever hoped for, had come to naught. He was a strong man, both physically and in courage and determination, but Helena had struck at his weakest point. He could not bear to be made to appear a fool.

'Sir,' said one of the maids, coming from the direction of the kitchen, 'Mrs Radford is still out. Cook wants to know if you'll be eating your midday dinner now.'

Harry had been working hard in the fresh air since an hour after sunrise, and he was hungry. This, in turn, faced him with a new problem. He did not wish to sit at the table with his wife, and neither did he want to provide the servants with fresh material for gossip.

'I won't wait for Mrs Radford,' he replied.

This being settled, he went upstairs to wash his hands and freshen up before going to the dining-room. He was descending the stairs again when Miss McPherson emerged from the linen room and spoke to him over the railings.

'Mr Radford, Mrs Radford has been out since before nine o'clock. It seems rather a long time.'

'I dare say she'll be home shortly for her midday dinner,' he answered, sensing a degree of reproof in the other's tone. He had gone down no more than three steps when the next disquietening thought struck him.

Where had Helena gone that she was so long? She did have the habit of riding alone, and he had occasionally scolded her for it. It was unlikely that she had decided to call on Ailsa over at Greyhills, and the day had turned so hot and oppressive that it seemed definitely peculiar that she would have stayed out so long. Had she suffered a fall?

Or...?

By her own admission, she had been thinking of suicide on that English spring day when he had approached her at the pond. Last night, he had taken this for dramatic trimming. Today, he recollected the sad and broken way in which she had uttered the words.

He forgot his hunger, and called out to Miss McPherson, who was returning to the linen room where she was whiling away the hot morning by tackling small mending chores.

'Did Mrs Radford say where she was going?'

'No, Mr Radford.' Miss McPherson was Highland and proud, and called no man 'sir'. 'She changed into her habit, and went out. I thought you knew about it.'

He sensed that it was no use discussing it further with Miss McPherson. She knew quite well that there had been a serious quarrel, and it was plain by her manner that she considered Mrs Radford was the injured party. Downstairs again, he encountered that same maid to whom he had spoken before, and she provided a clue.

That queer Mr Fisher, she said, had come to the back door asking for Mrs Radford, and Mrs Radford had spoken to him – when she could get a word in edgeways. Something about the Eggerts' farm.

Eggert's farm? What the devil!

He made up his mind without pause, and then walked rapidly from the house to seek out Frank Stott, the bookkeeper, who now resided, with his wife and young family, in the original homestead, and whom he knew to be checking on stores that day. Prince or no prince, the Garranbete routine had to be followed. A consignment of fine wines for the delectation of His Royal Highness's palate was of little use if any one of the thousand mundane items needed on a big pastoral property was unavailable when needed.

Stott was a quiet, steady man, and Harry knew that he could be trusted implicitly not to spread any unsavoury gossip.

'Frank,' he said, 'leave what you're doing. Mrs Radford went out riding hours ago and didn't come back. I think she's gone off towards Eggert's place.'

'She's a good horsewoman, and her mare's a reliable animal.'

'Still, accidents do happen.' Unspoken was his fear that when they found her it would be in circumstances which would betray that she had taken her own life. He added some explanation about Fisher, but pushed aside the other's suggestion that they should talk to Fisher first.

'He's three miles in the other direction, and once we start talking, we'll be all afternoon. You know what he's like.'

The two men rode across country towards the selector's small property, each watching out keenly for some sign either of Helena or the mare. They found the mare where

Helena had left her tethered, in the thick scrub bordering the road as it passed the Eggert property.

'Well, old girl,' said Harry, stopping to stroke the animal's nose, 'where's your mistress, eh?'

'We'd best go on to Eggert's shack,' suggested Frank Stott. 'He's away, I heard, but she's most likely still there. If "Dolly" mentioned that Mrs Eggert was sick, I'm sure that's the reason Mrs Radford rode over.'

'But why leave the horse there?'

Harry had no sooner asked the question than both men were startled by a rifle shot which cut through the sultry air and set cattle lowing and crows uttering their ugly cries as they fluttered against the sky.

Stephen Doyle climbed to the top of the nearest hummock, which gave him a command of both the low scrub behind the dune range and the wide beach, now being pounded sluggishly by the incoming tide.

The woman, Mrs Radford, had vanished. He had not been immediately behind her, but trying to cut her off when she had eluded him. As he stood there on his vantage point, scanning all which lay about him, he became very conscious of the powerful rays of the sun, only days from its solstice high point, pounding on his bare head and burning the fair skin which partnered his fiery hair. Under his shirt and jacket, perspiration itched against his skin, and he raised his free hand to wipe great droplets easing from his brow. He tried to see his quarry's footprints amidst the clumps of spiky grass which held the dunes together, but, unbeknown to him, the same fall which had whipped her from his sight had also caused sand to slide down over her tracks.

I should have killed her while I had the chance, he thought, instead of firing wide. Even as his mind worked on this, he knew that he could not have done so. The shots he had fired had been meant to scare her into stopping. Killing Mrs Radford meant killing Mrs Eggert as well. There was the baby. He did not wish to harm a baby.

I'm going, he decided. I'm getting out of this damned place. My presentiment up there in Ballarat was right. Mrs Radford *is* my evil fairy. If I stay, I'll be caught for killing the poor wretch in the woodshed. No wonder the Eggert girl seemed half out of her head. What woman wouldn't be after cutting her husband to pieces with an axe.

Major Doyle never at any time regarded himself as a murderer. He was a soldier, doing his duty. The old woman in Marseilles had been an accident. He had never considered himself actually responsible for her death.

But there was no doubt about it. His luck had never been the same since losing that rosary.

As there seemed to be no point in searching further for Mrs Radford, and anticipating that it would be some hours before she could, in stockinged feet – for he had found her discarded boots – find help, he began walking back towards the farm.

He'd saddle up, and at the last moment, loosen that wretched Eggert creature. Sooner or later, Mrs Radford would reach Garranbete, and spread the news about the mutilated body. He was sure of one thing. He would place as many miles as possible between himself and this misbegotten scheme. He was damned if he'd be condemned for a crime he had not committed.

Still watching out for Helena, he moved quietly and rapidly back the way he had come, trying to find his tracks through the low, mosquito-ridden scrub which tumbled down the inland side of the dunes. Parrots screeched away from him, and once a wallaby broke cover and bounded off in alarm, but he was in no mood for studying nature.

Holding his Winchester high, he waded across the river, finding it much deeper than before, because he had missed the ford along the line of the old fishtrap. He was nearly to the opposite shore when one foot caught in a hidden snag, and he tripped forward into the rotting branch which made this underwater hazard. As he struggled to regain his balance, his rifle discharged. The bullet sloughed through the flesh of his upper left arm, grazing the side of his chest at the same time.

The shock caused him to drop the rifle, and as he scrambled upright, he saw the bloodied swirls in the water drifting slowly downstream. He made one effort to recover his gun, but he knew that he had to bind his wound immediately, for the blood was spurting out vigorously. War experience had given him some knowledge of first aid, and he held his arm high, pressing into the pulse above the elbow with the fingers of his other hand. On the bank, gritting his teeth against the agony of his shattered bone and raw flesh, he managed to bind the wound with his scarf, clumsily, with one hand.

The distance from the farm, which he had covered so swiftly when in pursuit of Helena Radford, now seemed interminable, the gentle slope up from the river's edge like a mighty mountain. He was amidst the Eggerts' few cattle when he heard the horses. He ducked behind a bullock, and saw two men ride up to the shack, and dismount. It was with an effort that he choked back nervous laughter. So this was the place which Con O'Brien had sworn would be deserted, where no one would come except that simple-minded half-breed.

Even at this extremity, he did not lose his cool and shrewd judgement. He had one chance now – to sneak into the barn, somehow saddle up his horse and ride off. Briefly, he debated the chance of taking one of the new arrival's horses, but he did not desire to add horse stealing to his other troubles. There was bound to be some discussion between the two men and Mrs Eggert. If they found the body in the woodshed, and with the door wide open and in clear view, there was no reason why they should not, their attention would be sufficiently engaged to give him the chance.

His luck held. The luck of the Irish, he thought, bitterly, ten minutes later, as he galloped back towards Wicklow, but wide enough to miss that hamlet. He had to pray now that he could remain conscious until he reached his contact in Warnambool, twenty miles away, and that Con O'Brien had not betrayed him all along the line.

Harry Radford and Frank Stott turned in astonishment as the chestnut horse, whipped into an immediate canter, tore past with a white-faced man lying low on its back. Harry's first impulse was to give chase, but Stott caught his arm.

'We heard a shot, Mr Radford. He must be armed. It's better to find Mrs Radford before we think of anything else.'

Between them, they managed to drag a few coherent sentences out of Katie Eggert, who by this time was hysterical to the point of idiocy. To both her questioners, one thing was beyond argument. There had been a madman at work here, a maniac who, not content with slashing Wesley Eggert to death with his own axe and killing the dog, had settled down to torture two harmless women.

Harry rode in the direction Katie had

indicated, his heart cold and grim within him. We parted bad friends, he thought. Her behaviour was beyond forgiveness, but why did this have to happen after we had quarrelled so bitterly? He had heard a sermon about it once, when a travelling parson had stayed overnight at Garranbete, the old homestead, and had held a service the following morning. 'Let not the sun go down on your wrath', that was it.

'Lena!'

She stood on the opposite bank of the river, hatless, bootless, her clothing torn, and her brown hair lightened by the sand amidst the strands as it tumbled past her shoulders. Harry forced his horse to the other side, sprang down, and knew that she was comparatively unharmed. Her hands were scratched, and so was her face, but there was no other apparent sign of injury.

'Oh, Harry,' she said, 'I thought I was buried alive.'

Then, the effort for self preservation being no longer necessary, she let herself slip away into a dead faint. Harry bathed her face with water carried from the river in his hat, and when she had revived, there was nothing to do but allow her to rest awhile before taking her up before him on his horse's back. In response to his questioning, she told him something of what had happened, of how 'Dolly' Fisher had aroused her concern about the situation at Eggert's farm, and of Katie's strange behaviour, which had deepened, rather than allayed, her suspicions.

'You're lucky you're not dead,' Harry stated, tersely. 'Now, if you're up to it, Lena, we'll be on our way. I have to send someone for Constable Evans. With that madman roaming the countryside, the sooner people are on the watch-out the better.'

Helena held the palms of her hands against her temples. She was hardly yet able to view events with any degree of calmness, but there was now one thing of which she was sure.

'I don't think *he* killed Wesley Eggert,' she announced, in a low and still trembling voice. 'He was as shocked as I was myself. That's how I broke away from him.'

'Do you mean Katie Eggert – that little slip of a thing – was strong enough to do *that* to Wes Eggert?' Harry's voice expressed his disbelief. 'Then where does this fellow Doherty fit into it?'

Helena was right on one count, and wrong on another. Doyle, or as the Radfords knew

264

him, Sam Doherty, was certainly innocent of Eggert's murder, but Katie refused to take full blame for her husband's death. Katie loved Con O'Brien after a fashion, but she soon told her version of the story to Constable Evans.

She had been about to leave Wicklow with O'Brien when Eggert arrived, days earlier than expected. His reason was quite simple. He wanted to see the young Duke of Edinburgh, not having had the chance in Melbourne, for the Prince had already left on his country tour. As a result, the demoralised Katie and little Maria had been dragged back to the farm, but O'Brien was not so easily thwarted. The moon had not risen until after midnight, but as soon as there was sufficient light to see his way, O'Brien had driven almost to the farm, leaving his horse and buggy hidden in the roadside strip of dense bush.

By this time, it was near to dawn, and as Katie crept out, baby in arms, to join her lover, Eggert heard her. The two men began fighting in the pearly first rays of sunshine, and eventually, Eggert had reached the woodshed and grabbed his axe. O'Brien, a few years younger and certainly in a much better physical condition, wrested it from him, and less than two minutes later, Eggert was hideously dead, and his dog, which had rushed to defend him, a bloodstained mess of fur and flesh.

Even as O'Brien realised the horror of what he had done, he remembered that Fisher would be along shortly to attend to the stock. Somehow, he dragged Eggert, and the dog, into the shed, and removed as many traces from the dirt outside as he was able. The next action was to take Eggert's old horse from the barn and tether it for the time being in the scrub, away from the path Fisher was likely to take. This had hardly been accomplished when the guilty pair heard Fisher's cheerful whistle, and they hid in the shack until he had left.

O'Brien decided to bury the body, for he expected that his Irish-American acquaintance would be arriving later in the day. He had actually picked up the spade when he heard hoofbeats.

Doyle, confident that the farm would be deserted, had left Warnambool the night before, camped out, and reached the farm early with the expectation of putting in the day making his last minute preparations.

O'Brien, who had kept his head until now, saw only one way out of this new problem.

266

If Katie were in residence, he did not expect that the man he called Doherty would remain very long. He told Katie that the visitor was a travelling salesman named Doherty, and that she must act calmly. For himself, he would be off back to Wicklow, and give the impression that he had been there all night. He promised to be back in a few hours to collect her. So, whilst Doyle was stabling his horse, Con left the farm.

Of course, he underestimated 'Dolly' Fisher, whose keen ears had picked up a baby's hungry cry. He could not have anticipated, any more than Stephen Doyle did, that Mrs Radford, so far above the Eggerts both financially and socially, should that morning be eager to do anything to take her mind off her own problems. Thus, instead of sending a station hand, she had ridden over herself. A station hand might have been satisfied after speaking with Katie, but Mrs Radford was warmhearted as well as intelligent, and in a mood to fight against the wrongs meted out on woman-kind.

Conan O'Brien was duly arrested in Wicklow by Constable Evans. Privately, to Harry Radford, the policeman mentioned that he had fully intended to visit the Eggert farm that day. He had been absent most of the previous day searching unsuccessfully for an illicit still rumoured to be operating in the district, but he had heard on his return that Eggert had caught his unhappy wife with O'Brien in Wicklow. He was obliged to hold poor Mrs Eggert until a magistrate had sorted things out, and Mrs Evans could mind the baby for a while.

In reply to Evans' questioning about the mysterious Mr Doherty and his extra-ordinary actions, Conan O'Brien stuck firmly to his story that he knew the American only as a travelling salesman. Nothing made him budge from this, and even in his own extremity, O'Brien remained loyal to the Brotherhood's cause.

Katie screamed and protested as she was taken into custody, and removed, with O'Brien, to the lock-up at Warnambool. At the same time, the description of the man who called himself Sam Doherty was widely circulated, with the warning that he was dangerous and could attack women living alone.

Little Maria Eggert, innocent and un-knowing, was carried home to Garranbete by Helena Radford, to be placed in the care of one of the housemaids who came from a very large family and knew all about babies. At the last moment, Katie had implored Helena to take Maria, and rather to Harry's annoyance, his wife had agreed.

No one, except the loyal helper in Warnambool, knew that only two hundred yards from where Conan O'Brien and Katie Eggert sat in their separate cells, Stephen Doyle lay unconscious in a dingy back room.

And as the man who had given Doyle refuge hunted the public houses and grog shanties for a certain ex-naval surgeon who would do anything for cash and no questions asked, the deadly organisms of blood-poisoning multiplied and spread throughout the wounded man's body.

Nineteen

'Oh, you poor creature!'

No one would have thought that but two days since, Ailsa Radford had been so convulsed with envy that she had uttered the words which had left Harry Radford's marriage in ruins. Her concern was quite genuine. To be harried by a vicious man was the recurrent nightmare of every woman who lived in an isolated place, and even now, when so many of the old timber homesteads had been replaced by fine houses, the dread of being 'stuck up' by bandits still lingered.

To be just to Ailsa, who now rushed about giving every assistance, she had no true idea of what she had done. Her impulse had been to cut Helena down to size, and now with all the excitement and scandal of what had happened at Eggert's farm to talk about, she had virtually forgotten the earlier incident.

Helena was still at breakfast when the Robert Radfords arrived, and although pale and with her scratches stained yellow with iodine, she was composed. She had slept fairly well, mostly from exhaustion, and with the imminence of the royal picnic, had little time to think about her ordeal.

Harry thought carefully about her theory that Doherty had meant to attempt the assassination of the Prince. It seemed, on the surface of it, farfetched, and it was unlikely that Doherty would return to the area. However, one never knew with the mentally unbalanced, and he quietly arranged to have men posted strategically to keep a watch for suspect visitors.

He was also very thoughtful about Helena's miraculous escape by falling into a mysterious cellar in the sandhills. She had scrambled up a rough ladder, forcing her way though sand which poured down about her, and the more Harry considered it, the more he was convinced that she had inadvertently discovered his lost ship. There was something else, too, which she took from a pocket and showed him. During her blind gropings about her prison, her searching fingers had found and picked up this flat, round, cold object. It was a Spanish doubloon. Was this then the source of Eggert's income? Were those trips to Melbourne made for the purpose of selling, behind the law, old Spanish treasure? Harry warned his wife to keep this to herself. When he had the chance, he'd look for himself. 'Dolly' Fisher was going to look after Eggert's farm until affairs were settled, and no one could expect poor old 'Dolly' to cope with swarms of people out treasure-hunting.

To Helena, all this was a side issue. She was a woman, and to a woman affairs of the heart are all important. In novels, she had thought sadly that morning, as Miss McPherson helped her dress, the tragedy in which she had unwittingly become involved should have had the effect of bringing about a reconciliation between Harry and herself. But the rift was too deep, and the wrong she had done him too great. He had, of course, been relieved that she had come to no real harm, but although he had questioned her at length about what had happened, the coldness was still there.

On the surface, anyway, Garranbete had settled back into its customary well-organised calm, and the great day ebbed by without undue event.

During the late morning, Prince Alfred passed through Wicklow, which, according to one journalistic wit who described the scene, was half sober. This is, half the inhabitants were as sober as judges, and the other fifty per cent in an advanced state of intoxication. The two public houses were closed, but those enterprising persons who operated a still out in the bush had done very good business.

The local dignitary who represented Wicklow on the shire council had prepared a lengthy and high-flown speech of welcome, but the Prince's aides, already experienced in the ways of colonial orators, had quietly taken the address from the man's hands and given it to His Royal Highness, who then courteously thanked Wicklow for its warm welcome. The twenty-three year old Prince was now finding these occasions a great strain, and before the tour had ended, there would be considerable criticism of his impatience and unpunctuality.

There was one sour note in the Wicklow visit, and that was provided by the pupils from the Catholic school, who, like those from their National school rivals, had been drilled into deportment and neatness over several weeks. The National school pupils raised their large welcome banner, with its two crossed Union Jacks, as the Prince's coach drew near. Further along, as Wicklow petered out into cattle paddocks and potato patches, the Catholic pupils, in two lines with the taller at the back and the smaller at the front, also raised their banner. 'Give Ireland back her Parliament and set her Churches Free!', it read. The message was no stranger to members of the royal entourage, as it had been distributed on leaflets at many functions in Melbourne.

Then, as if to show that there was nothing personal about it, the young Irish

Australians burst into 'God Save the Queen', and Prince Alfred smiled and waved at them as he passed by in his well sprung Cobb and Co coach, drawn by the best horses the famous coaching company could muster.

The picnic was successful. The noticeable scratches on Helena's face and hands were explained as being from an unfortunate fall from her horse on the previous day. The Radford family felt that to reveal to the Prince or his aides the disturbing events which had taken place only a few miles away would be akin to lese-majesty.

So, in a great cloud of dust, Prince Alfred was borne off in his coach towards another several weeks of gruelling public life. When he had gone, the Radfords and their visitors took off their coats and loosened their stays (according to sex) and in their separate groups over alcoholic beverages or cups of tea (again according to sex) settled down to going over everything His Royal Highness had said, done, or eaten.

Some visitors stayed overnight, and it was late on the following afternoon before Helena and her husband had time for a private conversation. She was sitting before her bureau in the morning room, sorting out old letters, when she became aware that he was in the room, watching her. She said nothing, but continued her task.

'What are you doing?'

'I'm sorting out my old correspondence. Some of it is very trivial and not worth taking.'

'Lena.' A long pause followed, and when he spoke, his voice was strained and awkward. 'Lena, I'm not saying that things will ever be the same again but... Oh, damn it, Lena, I don't want to give Ailsa the satisfaction of crowing.'

'We could end up hating each other, Harry. It will always be there between us. I'm barren because I miscarried with another man's child. It's better to make the break now, before we become like – like the Eggerts.'

She was very busy with those letters, not looking at him, and he remembered, with an intense poignancy, the day of their marriage, when he had seen her tears reflected in the windows of their compartment.

'That's carrying it a bit far, isn't it, Lena? I reckon we're a cut above people like the Eggerts.'

She did not reply, and he placed a firm hand on her slight shoulder, feeling its warmth under the thin cotton of her summer dress.

'I'll write to old Revell again and tell him to disregard my last letter. Damned fool I was to write before I'd slept on it.'

'There's no need, Harry. I took the letter from the heap on the hall table. I don't know why. To give us time to think, perhaps. It didn't go. Here it is.'

She took the letter from a pigeon hole, and gave it to him, and then felt obliged to add an explanation.

'I forgot about it. So much else happened.'

He tore it up, and the pieces fluttered down into her wastepaper basket.

'Is it because I could have been killed that you've changed your mind?' It came out painfully. Helena did not want a compromise based on passing pity.

Harry sighed.

'It's not as simple as that, Lena, is it?'

She glanced up at him, directly, those beautiful, yet always veiled, eyes of her's swimming with tears.

There was nothing more that either of them could think to say. Both knew that repair work would be long and difficult, and yet, without discussing it, they were equally aware that they did not wish to live out the rest of their lives apart. He touched her shoulder again, and walked out of the room.

When he had gone, she sat very still for several minutes, staring down at her scratched hands and the rings that she wore. She felt sick with relief.

Twenty

Before many days had passed, Katherine June Eggert was released from custody, it having been found that she had no case to answer, although she was warned that she would be a witness for the prosecution in the forthcoming trial. At the same time, Conan Paul O'Brien was kept in prison awaiting trial for the murder of Wesley Eggert on the seventh day of December, 1867.

Katie did not return to Garranbete for little Maria, but went straight to Melbourne, where she temporarily disappeared from sight. Harry Radford was extremely annoyed, but Helena said that she was quite happy to keep the infant until such time as her mother's troubles were over and she was in a position to give her daughter a proper home.

The Radfords saw Prince Alfred again at the Christmas Eve Masquerade Ball in Melbourne, and this event marked the last high point in the Victorian part of the Australian tour. The Prince was by now becoming obviously less enthusiastic about the fulsome endeavours of his colonial hosts, and it was perhaps symbolic that on the night before his departure, a violent storm swept southern Victoria, quite wrecking all those arches and signs and transparencies which had decorated Melbourne since early November. The unalloyed praise from the public, too, had diminished. There were definite carpings about Prince Alfred's unpunctuality, spicy rumours about alleged calls on a notorious beauty who resided at a certain address in Stephen Street, and hints that the Prince's aides were not quite the stabilising moral influence they could have been.

That storm which whipped away so much of the festive evidence of the royal visit also cast up, on the wild coastline east of Warnambool, a man's body. It was noticed by a local farmer searching for a lost horse, lying on rocks far below. Here, the cliffs are striped like a huge layer cake, the savage waves chewing on them constantly, pulling chunks away from the mass to form islets, which over the ages have been worn into strange shapes on their way to final disintegration.

The body, recovered with great difficulty, was quite beyond recognition, although it was observed that the bone of the left upper arm was shattered. This coast had been the scene of many shipwrecks, and a small vessel having been reported missing recently, it was assumed that the dead man had been sailing on board her. He was buried not very far from where he had been found, and a wooden tablet was erected, bearing the date of the discovery, and the words 'An Unknown Mariner'. About two years later, the tablet was replaced by a stone cross of decidedly Celtic shape. There was some talk about it, because the person who paid for this did not reveal himself, but like all talk it eventually died away.

Conan O'Brien's trial received only minimal attention in the press, although there was one outstandingly dramatic moment when the widow, Katherine Eggert, having given her damning evidence under oath, turned to the prisoner in the dock, and cried out, 'Oh, Con, forgive me. I had to tell them because it was the truth!'

The prisoner looked towards his erstwhile mistress, and shook his head slowly, as if to say, 'It doesn't matter now.' In the end, the jury returned a verdict of guilty, not of murder, but of manslaughter, and he was sentenced to twenty years imprisonment. As he was led away, Katie screamed, and wept anew.

The newspapers had a better sensation than Conan O'Brien's trial that day. Prince Alfred was seriously wounded in an assassination attempt at a picnic near Sydney. A man named O'Farrell had rushed forward, and had managed one pistol shot before being overwhelmed by the outraged spectators. Shock waves of horror reverberated through the Australian colonies, and from thence throughout the British world. O'Farrell, who had a long record of mental instability, and should never have been released from that institution where he had been an inmate for some time, was rushed through a trial to the gallows.

During the weeks after Christmas, Harry Radford looked long and hard for the old ship, but no trace of it was ever found again. The sands, ever sliding, ever drifting, had concealed it too well. However, he did find the Winchester rifle, showing signs of weather, but still intact. As he looked down at that American wonder weapon, he really believed for the first time, that Helena's guess about Sam Doherty had been right. This was an assassin's tool, and as Harry imagined a hidden marksman emptying its magazine amidst the guests at the Garranbete picnic, he went cold all over.

He realised something else. The man who had brought this rifle all the way from the United States must have known how to use it to the best effect. When he had fired at Helena, he must have missed on purpose. Why?

Harry was not usually of a philosophical turn of mind, but he began to fancy that he saw his own place in the workings of destiny. If he had not met and married Helena – and if she had not been in a situation of great difficulty she would not have been at her father's home at that time – she would not have been here to circumvent what he was now sure had been a serious attempt on the life of the young Prince.

From the moment he started thinking this way, the wound, hidden but still bleeding, which he had carried inside of him ever since he had learnt the truth about Helena's miscarriage, began to heal.

The same night, without any fuss or talk about it, he moved back into the big room he had shared with his wife until their crisis. Later, counting back, Helena was sure that the first of their two children was conceived upon that occasion.

From time to time, there were rumours about Katie Eggert. Perhaps because she had been publicly exposed as an adulteress, she again vanished from sight. It was said that she had been glimpsed in the notorious bar next to the Theatre Royal in Melbourne, and someone else thought she had been seen, very painted and bedraggled, outside a dubious music hall. Nothing was done about the farm, which she now owned, for several months, and 'Dolly' Fisher, subsidised by a chagrined Harry Radford, continued to look after it.

One day, through instructions from a solicitor, the stock was sold off, and a letter arrived for Harry suggesting that he use the land for grazing purposes, free, as compensation for looking after little Maria.

'Good Lord,' he exclaimed. 'Run my good sheep on that place. They'd all go down with coastal disease.'

After a little more correspondence with the solicitor, an agreement was reached whereby a Wicklow labourer rented the shack, and another pastoralist ran a few cattle on the land. After this, small amounts arrived regularly for Maria. The whole thing irritated Harry enormously, and he frequently threatened to send the child off to an orphanage, a dire promise Helena knew that he would never put into effect.

Twelve months after the trial, Katie came to Garranbete unannounced. By this time, of course, little Maria was walking and talking, and very much the pet of the domestic staff. Katie arrived in a buggy with a smart horse between the shafts, driven by a soberly dressed man, who remained on the seat whilst his passenger sought out Helena. Hiding her astonishment, Helena greeted her as affably as she was able, at the same time studying her visitor. Katie's looks had improved. She was a little plumper, the hair beneath the bonnet was shining, and well brushed, and she was quite nicely dressed, if not in the latest style, yet neatly and becomingly.

Katie lost no time telling Helena what had happened to her during the past year, and it was far from the lurid life which gossip had sketched in for her. Immediately after the trial, in a state of almost complete mental and physical collapse, she had been taken into the home of a Methodist minister and his wife. For many weeks, they had treated her with the greatest kindness until, as she put it, 'she had found herself again.'

Since then, she had been employed as a domestic, but now she had come for Maria. For a long time, she had thought that her dearest baby would be better off where she was, but things had changed.

'Are you sure that you can care for her?' Helena knew that she could not deny Katie her child, especially as she now had one of her own, but she was still very dubious.

'Oh, yes, Mrs Radford. I've married a good man and he'll look after Maria like his own. He's out in the buggy waiting for us. Could I see her, please?'

So, feeling very sad, Helena introduced Maria to her natural mother, and helped her pack her clothes. Katie had brought a rag doll with her to help ease the parting, and Maria was soon happy to be going on what she thought was an ordinary outing. The man had left the buggy, and was now, to Helena's surprise, deep in conversation with one of the Chinese gardeners. When he heard them approaching, he turned and came to Maria, dropping on his knees before her, and talking gently to her until she rewarded him with a shy smile.

He was Chinese.

'This is my husband, John Lee,' said Katie, quickly and with a certain pride. 'We was married at Ballarat Methodist Chapel a week ago.'

Watching them drive away, and trying to subdue the ache she felt at losing Maria, Helena wondered why Katie had picked herself another problem. European wives of Chinese immigrants, even Christian converts, were considered beyond the pale by the rest of the Caucasian community. Still, he seemed a pleasant and decent young man, and she wished them both well.

After all, who could blame Katie for looking outside her own kind this time?

The publishers hope that this book has given you enjoyable reading. Large Print Books are especially designed to be as easy to see and hold as possible. If you wish a complete list of our books please ask at your local library or write directly to:

Dales Large Print Books
Magna House, Long Preston,
Skipton, North Yorkshire.
BD23 4ND

This Large Print Book, for people
who cannot read normal print,
is published under the auspices of

THE ULVERSCROFT FOUNDATION